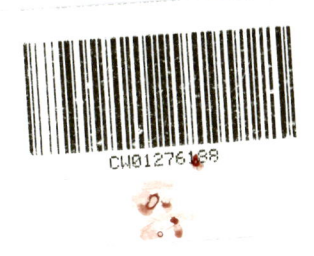

Moonshine

(The Moon Trilogy)

Book 3

Tim O'Rourke

Copyright © 2014 Tim O'Rourke

All rights reserved.

ISBN: 10: 150248868X
ISBN-13: 978-1502488688

Copyright 2014 by Tim O'Rourke

This book is a work of fiction. The names, characters, places, and incidents are products of the writer's imagination or have been used fictitiously and are not to be construed as real. Any resemblance to persons, living or dead, actual events, locales or organisations is entirely coincidental.

All rights are reserved. No part of this book may be used or reproduced in any manner whatsoever without the written permission from the author.

Story Editor
Lynda O'Rourke
Book cover designed by:
Tom O'Rourke
Copyright: Tom O'Rourke 2013
Edited by:
Carolyn M. Pinard
carolynpinardconsults@gmail.com
www.thesupernaturalbookeditor.com

For all of us who shine

Thanks to:

Shana at abookvacation.com
bookwormbetties.blogspot.com
Caroline Barker at Areadersreviewblog.wordpress.com
claricesbooknook.blogspot.co.uk
Melly at the Vampire Forum
Who all took the time to review my books – Thank you!

You can contact Tim O'Rourke at

www.kierahudson.com

Or by email at Kierahudson91@aol.com

More books by Tim O'Rourke

Kiera Hudson Series One

Vampire Shift (Kiera Hudson Series 1) Book 1
Vampire Wake (Kiera Hudson Series 1) Book 2
Vampire Hunt (Kiera Hudson Series 1) Book 3
Vampire Breed (Kiera Hudson Series 1) Book 4
Wolf House (Kiera Hudson Series 1) Book 5
Vampire Hollows (Kiera Hudson Series 1) Book 6

Kiera Hudson Series Two

Dead Flesh (Kiera Hudson Series 2) Book 1
Dead Night (Kiera Hudson Series 2) Book 2
Dead Angels (Kiera Hudson Series 2) Book 3
Dead Statues (Kiera Hudson Series 2) Book 4
Dead Seth (Kiera Hudson Series 2) Book 5
Dead Wolf (Kiera Hudson Series 2) Book 6
Dead Water (Kiera Hudson Series 2) Book 7
Dead Push (Kiera Hudson Series 2) Book 8
Dead Lost (Kiera Hudson Series 2) Book 9
Dead End (Kiera Hudson Series 2) Book 10

The Kiera Hudson Prequel Series

The Kiera Hudson Prequels (Book 1)
The Kiera Hudson Prequels (Book 2)

Kiera Hudson Series Three

The Creeping Men (Kiera Hudson Series Three) Book 1 Coming 2014!

The Jack Seth Novellas

Hollow Pit (Book One)
Seeking Cara (Book Two) Coming 2014!

Black Hill Farm (Books 1 & 2)

Black Hill Farm (Book 1)

Black Hill Farm: Andy's Diary (Book 2)
A Return to Black Hill Farm (Book 3) Coming 2014!

Sydney Hart Novels

Witch (A Sydney Hart Novel) Book 1
Yellow (A Sydney Hart Novel) Book 2
Raven (A Sydney Hart Novel) Book 3 Coming 2014!

The Doorways Trilogy

Doorways (Doorways Trilogy Book 1)
The League of Doorways (Doorways Trilogy Book 2)
The Queen of Doorways (Doorways Trilogy Book 3) Coming 2014!

Moon Trilogy

Moonlight (Moon Trilogy) Book 1
Moonbeam (Moon Trilogy) Book 2
Moonshine (Moon Trilogy) Book 3

Samantha Carter – Vampire Seeker Series

Vampire Seeker (Samantha Carter Series) Book 1
Vampire Flappers (Samantha Carter Series) Novella
The Vampire Watchmen (Samantha Carter) Book 2

The Tessa Dark Trilogy

Stilts (Book 1)
Zip (Book 2) Publishes October 2104

The Mechanic

The Mechanic

Unscathed

Written by Tim O'Rourke & C.J. Pinard

Flashes

Flashes (Book 1)

You can contact Tim O'Rourke at
www.kierahudson.com or by email at kierahudson91@aol.com

Moonshine

Part One

Winnie & Thaddeus

Prologue

"Where is the wolf's head?" Nicodemus screamed. "Why do I not have it already?" Blood dripped from his black eyes onto his pale face. The blood, the colour of his robes, filled the deep cracks and creases in his withering flesh.

"My brother, Lance, is doing his best, my Liege." Josef cowered before his master in the vast chamber beneath the Carpathian Mountains that twisted and stretched like a knotted spine over vast swathes of Central and Eastern Europe.

"His best!" Nicodemus cried in rage, clawing at the air just inches from Josef's face with his jagged claws. "The wolf is still alive – he is still breathing, even though my daughter is dead. Do you not understand my insufferable torment?"

Josef lowered his gaze; he couldn't look into his king's red, weeping eyes. It wasn't the grief or the hatred he couldn't bear to look upon, but the sheer fury he could see in them.

Snatching hold of his servant's face, Nicodemus sunk his broken fingernails into his pale flesh. "Look at me!" Nicodemus screeched. "Look. At. Me!"

Quivering, Josef looked into his master's eyes. They were so very black, he feared he might just be sucked deep into them and lost forever, swallowed up into his master's tortured soul. Josef could not see one glimmer – spark – of light in them. It was like his king's soul had gone to a place beyond death. He had seen the change in his master since he had renounced God – turned his back on the light and truly welcomed the darkness. It was as if God had now forgotten Nicodemus as much as Nicodemus had forgotten God.

"But the wolf has the Moonbeam," Josef whimpered, his master's claws burning deep against his narrow face. "He is protected by the light... it makes tracking him difficult. The light protects him. The light masks him from us."

"Don't talk to me of light!" Nicodemus cried as if in agonising pain. He pushed Josef away as if disgusted by his servant. "Any light in my life went out the moment that wolf took my precious daughter's life."

"But you turned your back on the one true light..." Josef dared remind him, his voice sounding nothing more than a whisper in the great stone chamber. The nearby candles flickered.

Hearing this, Nicodemus spun around, his purple robes flapping like great wings in the gloom and the shadows. "It is the one true light that has turned his back on me," he spat, blood flying from his lips. It was as if his grief was causing him to bleed internally – from deep inside. "It was Joseph of Arimathea and I who went to the tomb and prepared the corpse of the true light for burial. And where is God now that I have lost my daughter – my only child? Has he helped me prepare her body for burial like I helped prepare the body of his only son? No! I don't even have her body to bury – to lay to rest. The wolf turned her to ash. It is God who has abandoned me – not I, him. It was he who chose to take the light from my life. It is God who has left me in utter darkness..."

"But, my Liege," Josef quaked, pulling himself up into a kneeling position once more on the stone cold floor of the chamber. "You mustn't turn your back on..."

"I renounce him!" Nicodemus screamed, curling his long claws into fists and beating his chest. "I turn my back on him and the light. I welcome the darkness in my life – into my soul – and I will not rest until Frances's death is avenged. If I am to be punished, then so be it." Slowly, he turned his back on Josef. "God *can cause me no greater suffering than the pain I already feel." Snaking his dry, cracked tongue from the corner of his wrinkled mouth, he licked the bloody tears away that had gathered in the grooves there. With his back to his servant, Josef, he lowered his head. "Time is running out for you and your brother. Bring me the wolf's head, or I will go and claim it myself."*

Josef glanced up at Nicodemus, fearful of his master's threat. "But..."

"Don't fail me," Nicodemus warned, almost seeming to glide away across the chamber and disappearing into the shadows that gathered there.

"No, my Liege," Josef whispered, lowering his head once more, fearing that his king might soon be slicing it from his neck.

Chapter One

Thaddeus fed Winnie the last of the strips of meat. She licked greedily at them with the tip of her tongue. Her fever had begun to break as the blood from the meat started to satisfy the cravings that burnt deep within her. And even though the wind that rattled the tree branches above them was icy cold, a hot sweat glistened like a string of beads across Winnie's brow. With her cradled against his chest in the bushes at the side of the road, Thaddeus knew they had wasted too much time already. They had put little distance between them and the farmhouse they had just fled. If the two people he had seen approaching the farm through the darkness were vampires like Thaddeus feared them to be, he knew it wouldn't be long before they realised he had been there. With his free hand, he pulled the chink of moonbeam stone from his pocket. It glowed – pulsated – blue then white in the palm of his hand. It would blind the vampires to him, but in his pocket its protection was lessened. But Thaddeus feared wearing it in his ear like the earing it had been fashioned into. What had happened to him on the train stopped him from doing that. Wearing the moonbeam had changed him – turned him into the wolf that had lurked just beneath his skin for as long as he could remember, and that was dangerous. Not only because it drew attention to him and Winnie, but it was also dangerous to the humans. If he were to change fully – become the true wolf that he had to lock away during a full moon – then his killing would be bloody and indiscriminate. He had no control over the wolf once it was set free from within. On the train as Winnie had battled with her new and dark cravings, the moonbeam he had worn in his ear had made him part wolf. This he had always had some control over.

Since a boy, he had been able to release just enough of the wolf to protect himself and those who he had once loved. But it seemed wearing that tiny chip of the Moonbeam stone so close to his flesh had taken that control away – that ability to hold back the wolf and release it only when he needed or wanted to. *But why now?* he wondered, placing the piece of Moonbeam back into his jeans pocket. He scooped Winnie up into his arms and set off into the darkness once more. She made a soft whimper against his chest as he followed the curve of the road, making sure to keep to the shadows afforded by the treeline.

"Shhh," he whispered into her ear. "Rest."

But he knew Winnie was going to need more than rest. She was going to need someplace safe to sleep. Someplace out of the daylight that Thaddeus knew would be up in just a few short hours. Holding her tight to him, he pushed on. The road was remote and he had yet to see one solitary vehicle. Dare he try and thumb a lift? Would anyone stop for a bedraggled-looking man and feverish young girl? Someone might stop for Winnie, but she was too sick to stand on the roadside and wave a car down, even if there was one. The wolf inside him knew that if he had any chance of reaching Scotland and his *friend* Karl Lauderdale and the Moonbeam, then he should ditch the girl – give her up. But he couldn't – he wouldn't. He feared that Winnie would die without him. Others might die too if he wasn't there to help control her cravings. To help her turn fully from human to vampire. After all, he knew and felt some regret now that it was him who had made her a part of this world. A part of the dark world of shape-shifters and immortals he belonged to – was a part of. But it was a world – a life – that Thaddeus had lived for hundreds of years. And over those many centuries, he had grown used to and accustomed to the lust for human flesh and blood. He had developed ways of keeping the hunger at bay – he found places to lock himself away

– found people who he had trusted enough to keep the key safe to the prisons and the cells he had taken refuge in on each full moon. Now that job fell to Winnie. She would have to look after him as much as he would have to take care of her. They needed each other. Thaddeus, therefore, knew in his heart that he couldn't leave Winnie behind, even if he wanted to – because without her at his side, he risked dying as much as she. Whether she held him back or not, they were now forever linked – held together by the darkness that shrouded the world he lived in.

Just ahead, what looked like two round discs of light appeared in the darkness. They grew bigger with each passing moment. With Winnie still cradled in his arms and against his chest, Thaddeus watched from the darkness as the car approached. He could feel the heat of her fever radiating against him. With the engine of the car growing louder, Thaddeus looked east and could see the sky lightening there. Knowing that time was running out for him to find a place for Winnie to sleep and keep out of the approaching sunlight, Thaddeus stepped from the safety of his hiding place amongst the brambles and bushes and out into the road. With his back straight and Winnie in his arms, he screwed his eyes up at the glare of the approaching headlights. The vehicle began to slow. The headlights flashed brightly once, then twice. When Thaddeus failed to move off the road and out of the path of the approaching vehicle, another set of lights began to flash. But these weren't white, but blue and red and fixed to the roof of the car. It was as the vehicle pulled to a shuddering halt before him that Thaddeus saw the word POLICE written in blue across the hood of the car. The driver and passenger door flew open as two thickset police officers dressed all in black climbed from the police car.

"What's your problem?" the driver asked, sounding pissed off and disgruntled.

Before Thaddeus had a chance to say or do anything, the second cop was pulling his Taser from his overcrowded utility belt and aiming it squarely at Thaddeus.

"I recognise you," the cop said. "You're the poet who killed those three people, and then torched his own house."

Now also recognising who it was standing before them on the road, the other police officer yanked his Taser from his belt and aimed it at Thaddeus.

"Put the girl down and get on the ground, arsehole!" he ordered. Then, reaching for his radio with his free hand, he said into it, "All units, all units, I have located Mr. Thaddeus Blake."

Chapter Two

Detective Inspector Lance Stoke stood outside the farmhouse, mobile phone pressed to his ear. The reception from beneath the Carpathian Mountains was broken and weak, and the sound of the nagging wind made listening to his brother talk difficult. But he could hear enough of his brother's voice to know it sounded as fractured as the telephone signal. Glancing back over his shoulder, he watched Sergeant Becka Horton speak into her radio, summoning more officers to the scene to help deal with the slaughter of the male and female who sat gagged and bound at the farmhouse kitchen table. She turned away, against the wind, and as she did, Stoke glanced down at the swell of her arse in her black snug-fitting trousers. He imaged what it would feel like to sink his fangs into those soft mounds of flesh.

"Are you listening to me, brother?" Josef almost seemed to plead from the other end of the phone deep beneath the Carpathian Mountains.

"It's a bad line," Stoke said, turning his back on Becka and stepping around the side of the farmhouse. He wanted to take shelter from the wind, but more importantly, he wanted to be out of earshot from his colleague. Once out of the wind he said, "Tell Nicodemus…"

"No, you tell Nicodemus," his brother hissed, his voice sounding scratchy and far off. "I've never seen him like this. It's as if his grief – his fury – has consumed him. He wants the wolf's head…"

"I'm trying…" Lance snapped.

"Try harder," Josef almost screeched. "Because if you don't bring the head of that wolf back to the caverns, and soon, it will be us losing our heads."

With his blond hair flapping about the collar of his coat, Stoke stood stock-still. He knew that Nicodemus didn't make idle threats. He had seen his master slaughter his own before. It had been one reason Stoke had chosen to leave his home beneath the Carpathian Mountains and forge a life for himself above ground amongst the humans. It often seemed that those living too close to Nicodemus were living on borrowed time. He showed little forgiveness, and during the hundreds of years his beloved daughter Frances had spent living above ground with her wolf lover, his rage had only grown stronger and intensified. But on hearing of her death at the hands of the wolf, Thaddeus Blake, Stoke had at first believed he had discovered an opportunity to forever protect himself from his master's anger. If he was the one to return home with the wolf's head, then his life, until the end of time, would be safe. But now he wasn't so sure, and a part of him now wished that when his brother had asked him to track down the wolf, he hadn't taken the call. Blake was proving harder to find than he had first thought. In his arrogance, Stoke had wondered how hard it could possibly be to hunt down and kill the last remaining werewolf. Their race was on the brink of extinction. Blake was all that stood in the way of the Lycanthropes' total inhalation. But Stoke hadn't foreseen the Moonbeam. How could he have? How could he have possibly known that Blake would become in possession of a piece of it? But he had, and it was protecting him – shielding him from being hunted down and captured. Stoke knew that if he stood any chance of capturing the wolf, he would have to be just as cunning as the creature he now hunted. He glanced back around the side of the farmhouse, fearing that Becka might have come looking for him – that she might overhear his conversation. He watched her, bent against the wind as she continued to pass information to the control room about the dead mutilated couple at the farmhouse.

Josef spoke again in Stoke's ear, but he wasn't listening. He had zoned out again. Stoke was watching his sergeant Becka Horton from behind the wall of the farmhouse. He knew that she would slow him down – hold him back. If she knew what he truly was – if she were like him – then they could move faster – kill and feed on those who stood in their way, just like he had Blake's agent, Sarah Russell.

"Are you still there?" Josef hissed down the phone.

"Sorry, brother," Stoke said, slipping back around the side of the wall, deciding that he would either turn Becka Horton or kill her. "I'm doing my best. But the wolf has a shard of the moonbeam and its concealing him from me. I have to track him by conventional means and even that's proving to be difficult. This guy is really on the money. He doesn't use credit cards; he doesn't even own a credit card or drive a car. And now he's gone and half eaten a farmer and his missus..."

"But that's good, isn't it?" Josef asked, hope in his voice. "If he leaves a trail of corpses in his wake, then he'll be easier to follow..."

"No!" Stoke snapped. "It doesn't make it easier – it just muddies everything."

"How?" his brother asked, the howl of the wind unable to mask the sound of confusion in his voice.

"The more humans he kills, the more he will be hunted," Stoke began to explain. "That means more cops, and the more cops searching for him means that it might not be me who gets to him. The humans might capture him first. And what then? On the next full moon, locked up in prison or not, the humans are going to get one big fucking surprise. What happens when the humans finally have proof that immortals actually do exist? We know that Blake will do anything to save his scrawny neck. What if he makes a deal with the humans? What if he tells them about us? What if he leads them to our home? It has to be me who captures him – silences him – rips off his fucking head. Thaddeus Blake knows exactly what he's doing. Doesn't the realisation that he is the last of their race, but yet has still managed to survive hundreds of years, tell you something?"

"What?" Josef whispered, as if readying himself to share some sacred secret that might yet save his life.

"Blake is a survivor. He will do whatever, use whoever, kill whoever, pretend to love whoever, to stay alive," Stoke said. Hearing those words slip from his own mouth, Stoke now regretted once again ever taking up the bounty to hunt down the wolf. "That's how he has managed to survive while the rest of his race perished."

"So all is lost, then?" Josef breathed.

Stoke could hear the fear in his brother's voice as he once again glanced around the side of the wall in search of Becka. To his surprise, she was running toward him.

"Guv! Guv!" she gasped, dragging in lungfuls of cold, night air.

Stoke looked at her, the phone still at his ear. "What is it?" he asked her.

"We have him," she said. "A couple of cops have stopped Blake on a road about ten miles east from here."

"Get a car!" Stoke snapped at her. He watched her run back toward the police cars that were now heading down the lane toward the farm, lighting up the night sky in flashes of blue and red. Speaking into the phone again, he smiled and said, "Perhaps all is not lost, brother."

Chapter Three

"Put the girl down!" the police officer ordered Thaddeus again, his Taser still trained on him.

Clutching Winnie to his chest, Thaddeus glanced left and could see the second cop creeping around to the side of him. He too had his Taser aimed at Thaddeus.

"My friend is unwell," Thaddeus said, wondering how he was going to get away from the officers. He knew he could. It would be easy enough. But he didn't want to kill them if he could help it.

"Put the girl down and get on your knees!" the officer roared. He took a step closer.

Bending at the waist, Thaddeus slowly lowered Winnie down onto the centre of the road. Her skin looked almost translucent in the headlamps of the police car. Her long eyelashes flickered open then closed.

"Thad, don't leave me."

"Everything is going to be okay," he whispered in her ear.

Standing again, he looked squarely at the police officers. "Please, you really don't want to do this," he said, raising his hands slowly in the air. He could feel his claws pressing against his fingernails, desperate to be freed. He resisted the temptation to change. He wanted to find another way if he could. Killing two cops wouldn't be cool – not if he didn't have to. The hair beneath his flesh began to bristle, and his heart raced.

"On the ground!" the cop off to his left roared.

"Listen to me..." Thaddeus started, but before he could finish, the cop had begun to yell.

"Taser! Taser! Taser!"

Thaddeus felt his body suddenly go rigid – lock up – as if suffering from a series of violent spasms. A line of pain burnt horizontally across his chest. As his knees buckled beneath him, Thaddeus glanced down and could see what looked like two metal fish hooks attached to wires sticking out from his chest. He toppled forward, crashing down onto the road. He howled in pain. It felt like the electric shock he'd received was never going to lessen or fade away. With one side of his face pressed flat against the tarmac, he could see the second cop come running toward him.

"Leave him alone," someone said.

Scraping his cheek across the gravel, the pain in his chest now subsiding, he looked in the direction of the voice. Winnie was now standing, her back to the bonnet of the car. The headlamps stretched her shadow across the road like a black puddle of tar. In her hand she held the gun Thaddeus had given to her – the gun he had shot her with – the same gun she had tried to kill him with, but had been unable to do so because of the feelings of love that had grown inside her for him. The gun wavered from side to side in her weak grip. She steadied it by placing her second hand on the butt of the gun.

"I said, leave him alone." She stepped away from the car as both police officers looked back at her. Seeing the gun, they both lowered their Tasers.

"Now stay cool," one of the officers said, watching Winnie shuffle across the centreline of the road toward her friend, who was still lying face first on the ground, wires trailing from him. The further she moved from the car, the more she stepped into the light from the headlamps. From street level, Thaddeus could see that Winnie's usually fiery red hair was now black and it blew about her shoulders. Her skin was corpse-white, lips blood red. But it was her eyes, and he couldn't help but think of Frances as he looked into them. They were no longer green, but bright – almost a luminous shade of blue – that Frances's eyes had glowed when in her vampire form.

"Drop those things," Winnie said, looking at the Tasers the officers still held in their fists. As she opened her mouth to speak, Thaddeus could see the two fangs protruding from the gums at the top two corners of her mouth. They glistened in the red flashing lights atop of the police car, giving the appearance that her mouth was full of blood. "I said, put them down."

The police officers, looking at the gun held in her hands, then at her fangs, threw their Tasers aside. Their plastic shells clattered against the road as they spun away. Pulling himself up, Thaddeus made a grunting sound deep in the back of his throat as he pulled the metal prongs from his chest. He stood up, and as he did, he thought he saw a sudden fleeting movement in the bushes that lined the side of the remote road. The wind gusted hard and the tree branches overhead made a whispering sound. A deer skipped from out of the undergrowth further down the road, and then bounded away into the fading night. Knowing that the sun was creeping up on the horizon, he ran toward Winnie, who still had the gun aimed at the cops in her wavering hands.

"Are you okay?" he asked her.

"No, I feel like death warmed up," Winnie croaked.

"Couldn't have said it better myself," Thaddeus whispered, turning away and looking back at the two cops. They stood with their hands raised. Thaddeus snatched the speed-cuffs from the utility belt of the first cop he came to.

"You won't get away with this," the cop tried to reason with him. "Why not stop running now..."

"Not my style," Thaddeus said, spinning the cop round and forcing him to stoop forward.

Pulling the officer's arms behind his back, Thaddeus snapped the cuffs over each of his wrists. He yanked down hard on the piece of plastic-covered metal between each cuff to make sure they were secured tightly. The police officer cried out in pain as the metal scraped against the bones in his wrists. Thaddeus pulled the cop back into a standing position, then headed toward the other who stood nearby, Winnie's gun still trained at his chest. Again, Thaddeus took the cuffs, but this time placed them over the cop's wrists with his hands to the front. Winnie watched him work, her face, although white, feeling red-hot. She could feel a thick trickle of sweat run from her temple and down the length of her face like a tear. Her stomach felt like it had been tied into knots, and she knew that only more of the red, sticky meat that Thaddeus had been feeding her would unravel them. She twitched and her hands shook as she gripped the gun tighter in her fists. How could such a small thing feel so heavy? Winnie felt tired and weak; undernourished somehow. She swallowed hard, trying to rid the back of her throat from the burning sensation that was there. It felt like she had been choking on bile. Winnie could see the sky lightening in the distance, and her skin began to prickle like she had fallen into a bush of stinging nettles. The thought of the sun on her skin made her feel sick. It made her feel tired – like it was sapping her last remaining strands of strength.

"Hurry," she whispered to Thaddeus, fearing she might just collapse at any moment.

Glancing back over his shoulder at her, Thaddeus led the cop he had handcuffed to the rear, toward the thick bushes and shrubs that lined the side of the road. He disappeared into them with the cop, both disappearing from view. She looked back at the other police officer. He stood in the glare of the headlamps, the numbers on his epaulettes glistening like stars.

"Why don't you just let me out of these cuffs," the police officer half smiled at her. "We can figure this whole thing out."

"Shut up," Winnie said weakly, waving the gun at him.

The police officer sensed that perhaps she was losing her resolve – that perhaps she was the weakest link. Perhaps while her friend was gone, he could make her see sense and give it up.

"I know you wouldn't really shoot anyone with that," he said, glancing down at the gun, then back at her.

"Wouldn't I?" Winnie said, trying to keep her voice sounding strong and determined, even though she felt like curling up in a ball and letting the darkness take her. She thought of how she had shot the vampire Nate Varna in the face, scattering his brains all over Thaddeus. Varna hadn't been human, so did that kill really count? But all the same, she had killed to save Thaddeus, and she knew she would kill to protect him again if she had to.

There was a rustling from behind her. She saw the cop glance up, his face crestfallen, realising the opportunity to talk the girl into handing over the gun had now passed. Thaddeus stepped from the undergrowth, the cop's radio swinging from his fist. He dropped to the ground then stomped on it with his boot. The sound of breaking was like that of brittle bones as it shattered beneath his foot. Thaddeus strode toward Winnie, taking the gun from her hands.

"Get into the car," he told her.

Turning, Winnie shuffled back toward the car where she heaved open the back door. With her long, pale fingers gripping the door handle, she froze at the sight of a figure dressed in a red coat sitting in the backseat. A ruby coloured hood was pulled up over the face.

"Run, Winnie," a voice whispered from beneath the hood. "Run while you still can."

Winnie recognised the voice at once.

"Ruby?" she whispered. Winnie looked back at the road where Thad stood with the police officer. She wanted to call out to Thaddeus and ask if he could see Ruby, too, but when she glanced back into the car, her friend had gone. "Ruby?" she whispered again, crawling onto the backseat. She yanked the door closed behind her and lay down, her chest hitching up and down as she drew in shallow gasps of air.

"What have you done to my colleague?" the officer asked, as Thaddeus shoved him back across the road toward the car.

"He'll be all right," Thaddeus assured him. If Thaddeus could have left both coppers behind, he would've, but he couldn't drive and neither could Winnie. So he needed the officer for now. "Get in the car and drive."

"You're going to have to take off the cuffs," the officer warned. "How am I going to drive…?"

"Just get in," Thaddeus barked, the end of the gun poking the cop between the shoulder blades. He glanced over the cop's head and could see Winnie curled up on the backseat. With gun in one hand, he loosened one of the cuffs. The cop wriggled his hand free as Thaddeus quickly snapped the other cuff around the steering wheel. "Now you can drive," he told the cop.

Racing around the nose of the car, Thaddeus climbed into the passenger seat. "Now drive," he told the cop.

"Where?"

"Just drive," Thaddeus said. "Just keep off the main roads. Drive north until I tell you to stop." He waved the barrel of the gun just inches from the officer's face. "Go!"

The cop started the car and moved forward, picking up speed. Glancing back at Winnie, Thaddeus saw a black police issue coat lying in the foot well of the car. Snatching it up, he threw it over her, covering Winnie completely, just in case the sun came up before they found someplace to shelter for the day.

Chapter Four

Watching the cop from the corner of his eye, Thaddeus reached forward and turned up the volume of the police radio set into the dashboard. It crackled and hissed with static.

"How does this thing work?" he snapped.

"So you want me to drive and work the radio?" the cop said from the corner of his mouth. He shook the hand that gripped the wheel and the handcuff rattled. "You've got me cuffed up, remember?"

"Just tell me!" Thad said, his patience thinning. He didn't want to hurt the cop. Thaddeus could see the gold wedding band around the officer's left index finger. He had a wife and perhaps children. But the urge to let his claws tear free of his fists and cut the cop was growing with every passing moment. He didn't need to be jerked around – not now. He glanced back at the rear seat where Winnie lay huddled beneath the coat.

"The blue button," the cop said. "Press the blue button."

Reaching forward, Thaddeus pressed the button with his thumb. At once he threw his hands to his ears as the emergency sirens began to scream above his head, the lights flashed blue. The narrow road and the passing treeline lit up in strobes as if caught in a lightning storm. The police officer hoped that if any other police vehicles were nearby they would see and hear the pulsating emergency lights and sirens and know what direction he had been taken. Thaddeus hit the button with his fist, the plastic dashboard splintering under the force of the blow. The cop looked wide-eyed at the fractured dashboard and radio, then sideways at Thaddeus. Seeing his kidnapper's eyes now burning a fierce orange in the darkness, he lurched backwards in his seat, yanking on the steering wheel. The police car skidded across the road, back tyres screeching. Shooting out his arm, Thaddeus gripped the wheel and steadied the car. The cop looked down at the claw, then back at Thaddeus.

"Do you want to die?" Thaddeus roared at him, upper lip curling back in a snarl to reveal a gum full of jagged teeth.

"What are you?" the cop hitched, as if unable to breathe. He looked at the man who had taken him.

"Your worst fucking nightmare," Thaddeus breathed into his face. "Now listen to me very carefully."

The cop looked at him. Thad yanked the wheel as the car veered once again toward the ditch that ran alongside the road.

"Don't look at me, look at the road," Thaddeus growled.

With his mouth open as if still unable to breathe, the officer turned his head and stared at the road that snaked away into the dark. However hard he tried to fix his eyes on the centre white line, he had to fight the urge to glance to his right again at the monster that now occupied the car with him. Blake's hair appeared to have grown suddenly thicker – messier. His eye sockets looked as if they had been filled with molten lava. His hands had doubled in size and were curled into two giant claws. The cop couldn't help but notice that each long finger was capped with a razor-sharp hooked fingernail.

"You're going to kill me, aren't you?" he breathed. He felt the sudden need to pee.

"That depends on you," Thaddeus said. "Stop trying to jerk me about and I won't harm you. But I promise you this; if you go and pull another stunt like that, I won't think twice about ripping your fucking head off. Do you understand me?"

Looking front, the cop slowly nodded his head.

"I said, do you understand me?" Thaddeus screamed, pounding his fists into the dashboard again, as if driving home his point. The car shuddered all around them.

"Yes! Yes!" the cop tried to yell back, but his voice sounded cracked with fear. A damp, warm sensation began to spread out from the centre of his lap.

"Good," Thaddeus said, softer now. He settled back into his seat. He could smell the acrid waft of urine and he grinned to himself. "We have an understanding?"

"Yes," the cop mumbled again.

"The radio?" Thaddeus reminded him.

"You've broken it," the cop said.

"This radio," Thaddeus said, tearing free the radio that was fixed to the front of the cop's stab-resistant vest. It made a squawking sound in his fist. Winnie let out a groan from the backseat of the car, turning over in her sleep.

Winding down the window, Thaddeus tossed the radio out into the dark.

"Why did you do that?" the cop asked, daring to shoot Thaddeus a sideways glance.

"It looks too much like a mobile phone for my liking," Thaddeus told him. "And if it looks like a phone, it probably works like one, and that means it has GPS. Does it?"

The cop slowly nodded his head.

"And you didn't think to mention that fact?" Thaddeus asked him.

"I forgot," the cop lied.

"And I might forget I promised not to rip your throat out," Thaddeus warned him.

They drove in silence for several minutes. The cop couldn't help but notice how the wolf-like man kept looking back at the girl asleep on the backseat. He seemed to be distracted by her. That was good. The cop knew this part of the country well. He had policed it for the last eight years. He doubted the man knew it as well as he did. He had been told to keep to the country roads, but he knew if he headed east he would come to a more built-up area. If he could get there he might be able to draw attention, to raise the alarm, get some help.

"Head west," Thaddeus suddenly said as if able to read the cop's thoughts.

"West?" The cop shifted in his seat. His trousers felt damp and uncomfortable. If he were to survive this he wouldn't ever tell anyone that he had pissed his pants with fright. That was something he would take to the grave. How would he ever begin to explain what it was that had scared him so much? How would he ever be able to look his colleagues in the eyes and tell them some wolf-man had taken him hostage? He would be sent before the force medical examiner for psychiatric assessment. He knew that once you set off down that particular road, you were left to drift – your badge was taken away. He'd heard of a cop that got posted to some godforsaken town. She came back babbling about vampires. Her badge got taken from her and was never given back. No one ever heard of her again. It was like she'd disappeared.

"Yes, west," Thaddeus told him. "I want you to drive in the opposite direction of the sunrise. Find a place which is remote – a wood perhaps…?"

"But…" the cop started.

"Just do it!" Thaddeus barked.

The cop shifted in his seat again. Thaddeus could smell his fear. It emanated from the cop's lap. But Thaddeus knew, even though the cop was scared, he was smart. He had proved that with the radio stunt, by trying to hide the fact that it had GPS so could be tracked by the police control room, and the fact that he was heading toward the town of Black Rock. Thaddeus had seen the signs. Thaddeus saw everything. That's how he had survived for so long.

With the sun rising fast behind them, Thaddeus ordered the cop to drive faster in the opposite direction. The cop navigated the tight bends at speed, despite one hand being cuffed to the steering wheel. Thaddeus checked on Winnie again. She stirred restlessly beneath the coat. He glanced in the rear view mirror, the first pink rays of sunlight peeking over the tops of the trees behind them.

"Down there," Thaddeus suddenly snapped, pointing ahead.

"Down where?" the cop asked, stomach tightening. The well of fear that had been steadily bubbling away in the pit of his stomach lurched. Even though the road they travelled was remote, the narrow lane the creature was now pointing to would take them deep into nearby woods. From there he would be lost – lost to the creature and the restless girl with the gun.

"Are you blind?" Thaddeus asked. He knew the cop could see the lane. Was he starting to jerk him about again? Thaddeus hoped not. "There!"

The cop slowed the car and turned into the lane. Tree branches crowded overhead. They seemed to enclose the car, grab at its white shiny body – smother it. The police car rolled slowly forward, lurching and juddering as he passed over the rutted road beneath its wheels.

"Kill the headlights," Thaddeus said.

"But I won't be able to see," the cop protested. He didn't want to be in total darkness with the wolf-man.

"Switch them off," Thaddeus warned, turning in the darkness to look sideways at the cop, his eyes burning bright like firelight.

The cop did as he was told. In pitch-black, the wolf's eyes lit the interior of the car in a red fiery glow. "I can see," Thaddeus said. "Drive slowly. Keep going straight."

The car bounced as it left the road. Twisted black branches clawed at the windscreen and scraped down the sides of the car as they headed deep into the woods. Thaddeus glanced left and right through the windows. When he was sure they were far away from the road and hidden from view amongst the trees, he turned to the cop and said, "Stop."

The cop killed the engine. The sudden silence was ear-piercing. The only sound the cop could hear was his own racing heart. Pushing open the door, Thaddeus climbed out, and ducking to avoid low-hanging branches, he headed around the front of the car. He opened the driver's door, and taking the handcuff key from his pocket, he reached inside. Thaddeus unfastened the cuff from around the steering wheel, and pulled the cop out.

"Are you going to let me go now?" the cop asked. He knew the answer, but fear had consumed him. He was asking the question for his wife and eight-month-old son. It was like they wanted to know if they were ever going to see him again.

"Tonight," Thaddeus said. "After my friend and I have rested."

"How do I know you're telling the truth?" he whispered, fear strangling him.

"You don't," Thaddeus said, forcing the cop's arms behind his back with his giant claws. He snapped the cuffs over the cop's wrists, so he was handcuffed from behind. With the cop bent forward at the waist, Thaddeus led him to the back of the car. He opened the boot. In the darkness he could see that the back of the car was filled with traffic cones, police signage, and two fluorescent coats. Reaching inside, Thaddeus pushed the clutter to one side, making a space big enough for the cop to curl up in.

"Get in," Thaddeus said, prodding the cop in the back with one hooked fingernail.

"But I suffer from claustrophobia," the cop whined.

"Tough luck," Thaddeus said. He knew the cop wouldn't suffocate despite his fear of small enclosures.

"But..."

Without waiting for the cop to finish, Thaddeus pushed him in the back with one long claw. The cop fell face first into the boot. Scooping up his legs with both arms, Thaddeus seemed to almost fold the police officer in half as he wedged him inside.

"Please," Thaddeus heard the cop cry out as he slammed the boot shut.

Thaddeus walked away, the muffled cries of the police officer ringing in his ears. Using his claws like knives, he cut away some of the nearby branches and undergrowth. He laid them over the windshield and propped them against the car windows. He did this not only to hide the car, but to block out any sunlight that might filter through the leafy canopy overhead. Climbing inside, Thaddeus closed the door behind him, then crawled onto the backseat. Sliding one arm beneath Winnie, he pulled her close beneath the coat and closed his ears. Thaddeus let sleep take him as he lay and listened to the cop banging against the boot of the car, crying out that he couldn't breathe.

Chapter Five

Sergeant Becka Horton drove the police car she had commandeered through the brightening dawn. Detective Inspector Lance Stoke sat beside her. She glanced at him, and couldn't help but notice his face looked ashen, but his eyes were bright. He seemed pumped up – excited somehow. She could sense it, even though he sat rigidly still in the passenger seat studying the road ahead. She wondered if the sight of those dead people in the farmhouse had disturbed him somehow. But he was a seasoned detective, hardened by such sights throughout his career, she thought. It hadn't bothered her. In fact, the sight of so much blood had excited her deep in the pit of her stomach. The smell of the torn strips of human flesh laid out on the chopping board on the kitchen table had made her head swim, like opening a bottle of red wine that had a good nose. How she would've liked to have tasted it. Dropped a thin slither of that flesh into her mouth. Enjoyed the feeling of it sliding hot down the back of her throat. But not yet. Not now. It was too soon. She would have to keep her mask on for now. She glanced at Stoke again, knowing that he would eventually slow her down. That before they captured Thaddeus Blake and the girl he travelled with, she would have to kill Stoke. It would be easy. She knew that he wanted her. She had seen him more than once look at her tits pressing tight against the blouses she wore. Becka knew Stoke had imagined holding them, kissing them. But that's why killing human men was so easy. They were so freaking weak. A nice firm arse and a pert pair of tits and men seemed to weaken somehow – leave themselves open and vulnerable. Easy to kill. But she sensed too that there was something different about Stoke. Perhaps an inner hardness and strength. A cunning that would make killing him all the more exciting for her.

She peered into the distance, the first rays of morning light creeping through the tree branches that lined the deserted road they sped along. Stoke saw them too and it made his skin tighten – prickle as if covered with gooseflesh. He had hoped they would have caught up with Thaddeus before daybreak. The garbled radio messages had suggested that the wolf was close – closer than he now thought. He knew that the only way he would survive the first rays of sunlight was if he were to take human blood. It would stop him burning up for a few hours – until he managed to find somewhere to haul up, keep out of the light until nightfall. He studied Becka from the corner of his eye. Her pretty face looked taught, hazel eyes sharp as she navigated the tight bending roads at speed. Should he take her now? Rip her fucking throat out. Kill her like he had Sarah Russell and so many others. No. He couldn't. Not yet. If he were to kill her now, his colleagues would wonder what had happened to her. Cops don't just disappear. And if they do, no stone is left unturned until they are found again. Suspicion would fall on him and he couldn't have that. He couldn't be delayed in ensnaring the wolf. Both he and his brother's lives now depended on the capture of it. Once his prize was near he could kill Becka Horton without fear or worry. He wouldn't be around to be questioned. Stoke knew that it was time to move on again. Start someplace new like he had hundreds of times before over the centuries. But first he would capture and kill the wolf and take its head back to his master below the Carpathian Mountains.

He glanced at Becka again and knew he actually wasn't so sure that he did want to kill her. He *liked* her. Stoke knew that if he could, he would turn her. Make her like him. Make her his bride. Not many of the hundreds of women he had taken to his bed over the years had failed to give themselves to him. And he knew it wasn't his exceptional abilities at lovemaking that seduced them – it was the promise of immortality that did that. Who wouldn't want to live forever? Most human women did. Christ, it was just so fucking easy, he smiled.

"Stop!" he suddenly yelled, slamming one hand down onto the dashboard.

Pressing down hard on the brake, Becka brought the car to a juddering halt. "What's wrong?"

"What's that?" Stoke asked, pushing open the car door and stepping out into the fading night.

"What's what?" she said, going after him.

Stopping beside Stoke, they both looked down at the broken shards of black plastic scattered across the road. "It looks like a police radio," she said, hunkering down and prodding at a piece with her forefinger. She flipped it over and could see a name stencilled on the back. "It belongs to a Constable Crispin," she said, standing.

"The cop who radioed in stating that he had located Blake," Stoke said more to himself than Becka.

"He was double crewed, so that's two missing cops..." she started.

"And a police car," he said, striding away, and thrusting his hands into his trouser pockets in an attempt to shield them from the rising sun. The skin covering his face had started to feel tight and waxy – like a sheet of plastic pulled over his face like a mask. He knew he needed to get off the road and into some kind of shelter, and soon. Stoke looked back over his shoulder at Horton. She was kneeling again, her long, dark hair billowing back over her shoulders as she inspected some dark tyre marks left behind on the road. The urge to pounce on her, take her, sink his teeth into the soft flesh that covered the gentle curve of her neck was so suddenly overpowering that he had to force himself to turn away.

If he took her now, his thirst was such that he would kill her. He didn't want to do that. He had other plans for her. For the both of them. Lowering his head so that his long, blond fringe flopped over his brow, he thought he saw what looked like a boot sticking out from beneath a nearby clump of dense bushes. Glancing back once more and finding that Becka was still examining the road, he turned and headed into the bushes and undergrowth.

It was cooler – darker – amongst the wild brambles and thorns. He eased them aside and looked down at the cop who lay on his side. His knees were drawn up to his chest, and hands fastened with a pair of handcuffs behind his back. His clip-on-tie had been taken from around his neck and stuffed into his mouth. Stoke glanced back just once to make sure that he was alone, then knelt down beside the police officer. With eyes bulging almost out of their sockets, the cop looked at him. The fear Stoke could see in them excited him.

"There's no need to be afraid," Stoke said, smiling. "I'm one of you. I'm a cop." As if to prove the point he took his I.D. from his coat pocket and showed it to the officer. Once he had put the I.D. away, Stoke pulled the tie from the officer's mouth. He drew in deep gasps of air.

"I'm glad to see you," he wheezed. "Take these cuffs off. My arms are killing me."

"Let's talk first," Stoke smiled down at him, and he gently stroked the cheek of the officer's face with his thumb.

"Talk?" the cop frowned up at Stoke, flinching at his icy cold touch. "They're getting away."

"That's what I want to talk about," Stoke said, leaning over the uniformed officer. "Where did they go?"

"They took the car and..." he started to explain.

"They?" Stoke cut in.

"There was a girl with Blake. Looked about twenty. She had a gun. Waved it in our faces while her boyfriend handcuffed..."

"A gun?" Stoke mused. "And what did this girl look like?"

"She looked ill," the officer said a fresh sense of panic growing inside of him. He didn't like this Inspector. He was odd. He just wanted him to take the goddamn cuffs off. He could ask all the questions he wanted to later.

"Ill?"

"Yeah, like she had some kind of fever," the cop explained. "Can you just take these cuffs off...?"

"Shhh," Stoke said, pressing one long finger against the officer's lips. "What colour hair did this girl have? What colour were her eyes?"

The officer jerked his head back, away from Stoke's finger. The guy was fucking creepy. "She had black hair. Bright blue eyes..."

"Black hair? Blue eyes?" Stoke said thoughtfully. He had seen a picture of the girl who had fled London with Blake. An image captured on CCTV had been sent to his mobile phone from the British Transport Police. The girl in the picture had had red fiery hair. She had been described by witnesses as having bright green eyes. Nate Varna had got word back to the vampires still living beneath the Carpathian Mountains that the girl had looked identical to Frances – Nicodemus' daughter. Could Blake be traveling with another girl? Stoke wondered, looking down at the cop as if he had the answers he was searching for. Then Stoke remembered the reports he'd read from witnesses aboard the train. They had described the girl as freaking out. What if the girl Blake was traveling with had been bitten by a vampire... Nate, Michelle, or Claude? What if Blake was now traveling with a vampire? She would be going under her change. She would be sick, unpredictable, and very dangerous. Stoke knew that she would slow Blake down. She wouldn't be able to travel by day, just like he couldn't. So they wouldn't have gone far. They wouldn't be going anywhere until nightfall. And Stoke knew that if the girl had been bitten, then she was more like him than Blake. She was a vampire, and therefore could be turned against the man she had escaped with.

"Can you un-cuff me now?" the cop asked, prodding Stoke out of his thoughts.

Stoke looked down at him and took a pair of latex gloves from his coat pocket. They stretched like an extra layer of skin as he pulled them over his hands.

"Take these cuffs off," the copper grimaced, eyes wide as he watched Stoke take what looked like a bloodied butcher's apron from inside his coat and put it on. "Release me!"

"No," Stoke smiled, pushing the tie back into the officer's mouth. He made a gagging noise in the back of his throat. "I'm not going to untie you. I'm going to eat you," he said, snapping his head forward and sinking his teeth into the officer's throat.

Arming blood from his mouth, Stoke stepped from the bushes and back onto the road. The damp apron and sticky gloves were once again hidden in the deep pockets sewn into the inside of his long coat. He belched. His throat and mouth flooded with stringy pieces of flesh and blood. He swallowed them back down again. Becka was further down the road. The sun was almost up, the sky to the east a deep red. Hearing the sound of Stoke's boots on the tarmac, she glanced back over her shoulder, looking at him.

"Where did you disappear to?" she frowned.

"I thought I saw something in the bushes and the undergrowth back there," he said, gesturing over his shoulder. "But it was nothing. What about you? Did you find anything?"

"Nope," she said, sounding disappointed.

"I don't think they would have gone very far," he said. And just wanting to find a motel or bed and breakfast to rest up in, he quickly added, "I think we should head into town and find somewhere to get our heads down. We've been up all night."

"But the car… PC Crispin and the other…" she started.

"Let the local officers start the search, if they find either of the missing cops or the car, they will soon let us know," he said, turning his back on her heading toward the car. "I need to find some place to sleep."

Chapter Six

"Come with me, Winnie. I want to show you something," Ruby Little whispered in her friend's ear.

Winnie snapped open her eyes and sat up. It was still dark inside the car. Thaddeus and the cop had gone. He was no longer cuffed to the steering wheel. She was alone. It was cold, and a strong wind gusted into the car. The door to her right was open, and she could see Ruby Little standing just outside in the dark. Her hood was pulled up as always, her face masked in shadow. But all the same, Winnie thought that her friend's face seemed to move – writhe – shift from side to side, up and down, like the flesh was falling from her face.

"Winnie," Ruby whispered over the wind. She held out a small, delicate looking hand and beckoned her friend. "I want to show you something."

Sliding over the backseat of the police car, Winnie got out. She looked up, her bright blue eyes inspecting the wooded area she found herself in. Someone had covered the car in branches, twigs, and leaves. It looked just like another part of the bristling undergrowth in the wind. Winnie shuddered as she felt something cold and clammy enclose about her hand. She glanced down to see that Ruby Little had wrapped her fingers around it. She looked at her friend. And even though it was fully dark in the woods, she could now see beneath her friend's hood. It was as if she could see through the darkness now. She looked at her friend's small, round face and pulled backwards. Ruby held Winnie's hand firm as if not wanting to let her go – escape. Winnie recoiled at the sight of the maggots that had now infested Ruby's face. They crawled from her black eye sockets, her nostrils and mouth. It was like her face was alive.

"I need to show you something," Ruby whispered again, and as she spoke, maggots wriggled from the corners of her split, crusty lips. They dropped onto her blood-red coat like tiny lengths of pasta.

"What do you need to show me?" Winnie breathed deeply. She covered her mouth with her free hand. Not to stifle a scream, but the rancid smell of rotting flesh that wafted from her friend's face.

"This way," her friend said, pulling on her hand and leading her away from the abandoned police car and deep into the wood.

Foliage broke and snapped underfoot. It was so quiet that each breaking twig and branch sounded like gunfire in the darkness. They walked together in silence, maggots raining down from beneath Ruby's hood and onto the front of her coat. Winnie tried not to look at them, tried not to smell the rotting flesh they gorged themselves on.

"Why do you keep showing yourself to me?" Winnie asked her. "Why can't you just stay dead?"

"Because I need to show you stuff," Ruby told her, peeking out from around the edge of her hood. Her face looked like it was covered in rice.

Winnie looked away. "What stuff?" she whispered.

"I want you to see through the monster's eyes," Ruby said. "I want you to see what the monster sees."

"And what does it see?" Winnie asked, her now long, black hair blowing across her face.

"See through the creature's eyes," Ruby said, her hand falling away from Winnie's.

Winnie clawed the strands of long, black hair from her eyes. She was no longer in the woods, but standing looking at the farmhouse Thaddeus had led her to. The wooden sign attached to the farmhouse wall read *Sweetlands Farm*. She looked to her left and could see the barn where Thaddeus had hidden her. Where he had brought her those stringy lengths of meat. The meat that was so thick and sweet with blood. The meat that had satisfied the burning hunger that now raged deep inside her since being bitten by the vampire, Michelle.

Winnie looked back at the house. Once again she was alone. Ruby Little had deserted her once again. Then, as if looking through the eyes of another, Winnie slowly pushed open the front garden gate and approached the farmhouse. She wanted to stop dead in her tracks and turn back, but she couldn't. It was like she was now inside someone else – *something* else – looking out through its eyes – seeing what it saw. Seeing what it had done while she'd slept in the barn on the other side of the farm.

She brought her fist up and knocked on the door. Except it wasn't really her fist – it was the monster's. She knocked again. Winnie could hear movement on the other side of the door. A bolt being slid back. She wanted to scream out and tell whoever was opening the door not to do so. She could see into the monster's heart. She knew what it intended to do once inside the farmhouse. She could feel its hunger and it matched her own.

The door swung open. A bony man in his fifties stood in the open doorway. His face was lined and weather-beaten. Too many harsh winters spent working the fields – tending to his lambs. Winnie pitied him because she knew what the monster was going to do but she was helpless to stop it. She was trapped inside the monster's body.

"Hello," the farmer said. "Can I help you?"

"Me and a friend have become lost and we don't know the area," the monster said. "My friend is sleeping nearby, but I was wondering if you had any food that you could spare, as we're both very hungry and haven't eaten for days."

The farmer looked back at Winnie and she wondered why he wasn't screaming at the sight of the monster standing at his door. Then Winnie realised that the monster was still hidden, it hadn't shown itself yet to the farmer – that would come later – when the monster had gained the farmer's trust. The farmer couldn't see the monster's jagged teeth, claws, and billowing hair. But he soon would. Winnie could sense – *feel* – the monster's growing hunger.

"It's very late," the farmer said, looking back at a clock attached to the hallway wall. "It's gone ten."

"I don't mean to be a nuisance," the monster said. "But my friend isn't feeling well..."

"Who is it, John?" a voice called out from deep within the farmhouse.

A female voice, the monster noted. *More flesh,* the monster thought, and its heart raced.

Winnie wanted to scream out and warn the farmer to shut the door and lock it tight. But she couldn't. It was only the monster she now found herself in that had a voice.

"Someone who's got lost," the farmer hollered back.

"Lost?" A middle-aged woman wearing a floral patterned dress and a shawl appeared at the end of the hallway. She then saw the face of the monster and smiled. "Come in. Don't stand out there in the cold; you'll freeze."

"Thank you," Winnie heard the monster say, stepping inside. It passed the farmer and into the hallway.

John closed the front door and followed the monster into the kitchen. There was a fire burning in the stove. The monster warmed itself, rubbing the hands that would soon be claws together.

"Are you alone?" the woman asked.

"I have a friend who's not feeling too well," Winnie heard the monster say.

"Where are they?" the farmer asked.

"Sleeping," it said right back.

"What – out in the cold?" the woman frowned. "Go and get..."

"I just need some food, that's all..." the monster started.

"We don't have much..." she said.

"You have plenty," the monster said, eyeing the woman's voluptuous figure squeezed inside the pretty dress. The fire sparked in the stove. The woman glanced at it. That was all the time the monster needed. Just that one second. It leapt across the kitchen, claws springing from its fists, jagged teeth slicing out of its gums, hair billowing behind it. The creature could see itself reflected in the terrified eyes of the woman. It couldn't help but think itself to look beautiful. Glorious. Winnie closed her eyes inside the monster, but still she could see through its eyes, as it clawed the woman's throat open in a jet of red. She gargled. The farmer screamed, reaching for his shotgun. As the woman fell face first onto the kitchen table, the creature reached for the man, swiping the gun from his hands. Sliding its claw into the man's stomach, he yanked on his hot, slippery intestines.

When both were dead, the monster sat them at the kitchen table. It bound them to the chairs so they sat upright. The creature sat opposite the couple as if they were all about to have a meal. But only one of them would be eating. Using its claws, the creature began to slice thin strips of flesh from the warm corpses sitting up at the table.

"Isn't this nice?" the monster smiled, throwing back its head and dropping the first slither of meat into its mouth.

Winnie wanted to be free of the monster. Why had Ruby showed her this? Why had Ruby let her stare out from behind the creature's eyes? Who was the monster who'd done such a terrible thing? She had to get to the barn and warn her friend. She had to tell Thaddeus that a vampire was close by. They weren't safe in the barn. They had been discovered. She looked up through the eyes of the monster. Winnie could see that someone else had now joined her in the room. But who? She didn't know as they were hidden in the shadow of the hallway. Whoever they were, Winnie knew she and Thaddeus had been discovered. She knew they now had to run... they had to run... run... run...

"Have some of this," she heard someone whisper in her ear.

Winnie opened her eyes. She was back in the police car, lying beneath a coat. Thaddeus was beside her. In his fist he held what looked like several strips of bloodied flesh.

"Eat it," he whispered. "It will give you strength. It will sedate your thirst."

Chapter Seven

With the nightmare still fresh in her mind, Winnie turned her face from the piece of meat Thaddeus held to her dry lips.

"Eat it," Thaddeus coaxed her. "You'll need it to stay strong – stay alive."

"I thought I was dead already," Winnie groaned, her stomach somersaulting with hunger at the smell of the meat. She fought the urge to turn around and swallow down the meat Thaddeus was offering her.

"You're still going through your change," Thaddeus said, lowering his fist that held the meat. The smell of it, in the confines of the police car, was mouth-watering, even though he had eaten already. "If you don't eat, take fresh blood, you'll fade – turn to ash – just like Frances did. That's how vampires die. I had to watch Frances die, remember? And it was agony for the both of us. I can't watch you die the same way."

"Why not?" Winnie asked, that nightmare still at the forefront of her mind. She closed her eyes, but that just made the images of the dead couple sitting sliced to pieces at the kitchen table even more vivid.

"You know I care for you, Winnie..." Thaddeus started.

"Is that all?" she said, knowing that her feelings for him were stronger than just simply caring. The knowledge that when she'd tried to shoot him in the barn and the gun had failed, proved that she cared deeply – loved him even.

"You know I would do anything to protect you," Thaddeus said.

"Would you kill for me?" Winnie asked, opening her eyes and looking at him in the gloom of the car.

Thaddeus looked into her eyes that had now returned once again to their bright green colour. "You know I killed Michelle, Claude..."

"Humans, I mean," she cut in.

"If it meant saving you, then yes," Thaddeus nodded.

"To feed me?" she asked, wanting to know if it had been his eyes she had been seeing through in her nightmare.

"What's that meant to mean?" he said.

"I had a nightmare..." she started but trailed off, fearing now that she might sound paranoid – suspicious of him.

"What did you see in this nightmare?" Thaddeus asked.

"I'm not sure if it was a nightmare or perhaps a vision of some kind," she tried hard to explain, her mind feeling foggy now that she was awake.

"A vision?" Thaddeus asked, still holding the strips of flesh in his fist. Winnie couldn't help notice how the blood from it trickled through his fingers in sticky black streams. She wanted desperately to suck the blood from his fingers. She looked away, her stomach in fiery knots of hunger. She noticed for the first time since waking that the police officer had gone and the windscreen was covered in branches, just like in her dream.

"Ruby Little was here..." Winnie started.

"But your friend is dead," Thaddeus reminded her.

"I see her all the time," Winnie finally confessed. "I saw her first back at your house... the night you left me alone and the vampires came. I saw her at Sarah Russell's house, then again at the station and on the train. Her face is rotting beneath the red hood of her coat. It's like she's come back from the dead to give me some kind of warning."

"Warning?" Thaddeus said, remembering how he thought he had seen a girl wearing a red coat in the barn they had hid in. "What kind of warning?"

Winnie stared at him – looked hard into his nearly black eyes. "I think Ruby is trying to warn me away from you. She keeps telling me I should run from you."

"But why?" Thaddeus asked. "I haven't hurt you."

"Apart from deceiving me into coming to live with you at your home, leaving me alone to defend myself against a pack of bloodthirsty vampires, forgetting to tell me that you're a werewolf, and then shooting me – nah, you've not hurt me, Thaddeus," Winnie said.

"What I meant was, I haven't tried to kill you," he said back, looking a little hurt. "Okay, so things didn't work out how I intended them, my plan went wrong..."

"Wrong!" Winnie scoffed. "It's been a complete and utter fuck-up from start to finish."

"You're still alive, aren't you?" He tried to defend himself.

"Am I?" Winnie sighed. "I'm turning into a vampire."

"What I'm trying to say is that I could have left you behind," he started to explain. "But I didn't. I stayed with you. Brought you with me, even though you've slowed me down – I could have been in Scotland by now. I could have the Moonbeam."

"*Soreeey!*" Winnie snapped.

"That's not what I meant," he sighed.

"So you keep saying," she shot back. "So what is it you do actually mean?"

"I brought you with me because I feel responsible about what happened to you..." Thaddeus tried to explain.

"I ain't no charity case," Winnie snapped, reaching for the car door handle and wanting to get out. The atmosphere in the car had suddenly become hot and oppressive.

Shooting his arm out, Thaddeus grabbed her, pulling her around to face him.

"I can look after myself," Winnie said. "I've had years of practice…"

"Why don't you shut up," Thaddeus said. Then, leaning forward, he pressed his lips hard against hers.

Winnie struggled momentarily against him, but slowly weakened as his kiss grew more intense and deeper. She kissed him back and could taste blood. Winnie knew then that he had recently eaten. She slid her tongue over his. Just wanting more of him – more of the blood she could taste on him.

Slowly, he broke their kiss. With his eyes still locked with hers, Thaddeus said, "It's difficult for me to say this, Winnie, as I feel I'm betraying someone I loved deeply for centuries… I feel guilty…" he trailed off.

"What is it?" she asked. "What do you have to feel guilty about?"

Thaddeus swallowed hard. "I'm falling in love with you," he said. "I never meant to. It was never part of the plan. Every time I look at you – every time I take your hands in mine – every time we kiss, I feel guilty. I feel that I'm betraying Frances somehow."

Winnie was shocked by his sudden confession. They both sat in silence. She had never wanted to replace Frances. Had never intended on falling in love with Thaddeus. That hadn't been part of her plan, either. Hers had been to escape the streets of London. Make a better life for herself. Start anew. But Winnie knew she had fallen in love with Thaddeus and she couldn't turn off those feelings or pretend they weren't real any longer.

"Would she have wanted you to spend the rest of eternity alone?" Winnie suddenly broke the silence. "I wouldn't want that for someone I loved. I'd want them to be happy."

"It doesn't matter what Frances might have wanted for me, it's what I want that troubles me," he said.

"And what do you want?" Winnie asked.

"You," he said, glancing at her. "But I've loved twice before. First there was Revekka, and I got her killed by trying to seek revenge on my aunt and cousin, Dominika, for stealing the Moonbeam. Then there was Frances, and I ended up killing her with a bite. So maybe your friend Ruby Little is right, and you should run as far from me as you can."

Winnie looked down at the strips of meat still clutched in his hands. Black spots had appeared on his blue jeans where blood had dripped onto them. Without looking up at him, but staring at the strips of red meat, she said, "Did you kill for me back at the farm? Did you kill the owners of that place to feed me?"

"Who told you such a thing?" Thaddeus asked, sucking in air.

"Did you?" This time Winnie did match his stare. She needed to know if it was his eyes Ruby Little had made her look through.

"The only living thing I killed back at the farm was a lamb, and that was so I could feed you," he said, his eyes clouding over with hurt.

"And what kind of meat is that?" Winnie asked glancing back down at his fist then back at him.

"It's fucking deer meat," he said, throwing it against the dashboard. Smearing blood from the palm of his hand, Thaddeus pushed open the car door and climbed out. Winnie sat in silence, watching the meat slide down the dashboard in wet chunks. Sliding from the seat, she climbed out. Thaddeus stood near the boot of the car, his back to her.

"I'm sorry," she said, reaching out and placing one hand gently on his shoulder.

He shrugged it off. "I'm sorry you think so little of me."

"That's not true," she said.

Thaddeus turned to face her, his eyes completely black. "My whole life I've spent being locked away so that I didn't hurt humans," he said. "I'm not the monster you obviously think I am."

"I don't think you're a monster," Winnie said, now full of guilt. "I'm just confused. I'm trying to make sense of everything. I'm trying to make sense of..." she trailed off.

"What?" he pushed.

"The fact that I've gone and fallen in love with a monster," she half smiled at him.

Taking a deep breath, Thaddeus said, "You're not the only one."

They looked at each other in the darkness. Winnie wanted to take back what she had said. But she couldn't. "Friends?" she asked, holding out her hand for him to take.

"More than friends," he said, taking her hand in his and pulling her close. Resting his head against her soft hair, he whispered, "I'm so sorry for everything I've done to you, Winnie."

Holding him tight, she whispered back, "Do you have any more of that meat? I'm starving."

They sat together in the car and ate the rest of the meat Thaddeus had hunted. When there was nothing left, Winnie licked the blood from her hands and between her fingers.

"Feeling better?" Thaddeus asked her.

"Better," she nodded.

"Good," he smiled, "because we need to get going. The cops are going to be looking for this car and we need to be far away from here."

Winnie clambered from the back of the police car, then frowning, she said, "What happened to the police officer – the one who drove us out here?"

"You don't remember?" he asked.

"Remember what?" she said with a shrug.

"I cut him loose just before I woke you," Thaddeus said.

"That's a bit risky, wasn't it?"

"And that's why we need to get going," he said, turning once more in front of her.

She looked at him, claws swinging low, eyes shining brightly in the dark and mouth full of jagged teeth. Winnie knew that if she were going to keep up with him – stand any chance of outrunning the police that the other cop would bring back with him, she would have to let loose her inner monster too. As if being able to sense her hesitation – her fear – Thaddeus said, "Don't be scared of it. Get to know it. It's a part of you now. That's the only way you'll ever be able to control it."

Screwing her eyes shut tight, Winnie concentrated on that other self – that creature that now lurked deep inside her. She could feel it there, just beneath her skin – like a twin. Her body suddenly began to cool, like she had been plunged beneath cold water. The feeling made her skin tingle, and although she knew she was dead, she suddenly felt more alive than she ever had. Rolling her tongue around in her mouth, she felt the fangs that now protruded from her gums. Winnie felt her fingers stretching, and at first she wondered if Thaddeus hadn't suddenly stepped forward through the dark and grabbed her hands. She opened her eyes but he hadn't moved. The darkness seemed lighter now. It was as if the night had radiance to it. Glowed somehow. Raising her hands to her face, Winnie inspected the claws that were now there. Her fingers were white as bone, long and slender with black razor-sharp nails. The wind blew her thick, long hair from her shoulders and it was the colour of raven's wings.

"You look beautiful," Thaddeus said, taking a step toward her.

"Do I?" she asked, still needing to be convinced.

"More beautiful than anything," he said.

More beautiful than either Revekka or Frances? she wanted to ask, but she didn't.

"Look," Thaddeus said, gently turning her by the shoulders. She caught sight of her reflection in the car window. It was her eyes that grabbed her attention first. They were such a bright blue, they almost seemed to illuminate the darkness all around them. Her hair, although black, shone too, as did her white pearly skin. Snaking his arm about her waist, Thaddeus pulled her to him. Pressed tight together in each other's arms, he softly kissed her deep, red lips.

Was he kissing her or Frances? Winnie wondered. But she pushed those insecurities away. She wasn't Frances. Her name was Winter McCall. And for the first time in her life, she was awake – like she had been reborn. Like she had the skin of her old self and stepped out into the night anew.

Breaking their kiss, Thaddeus pulled the gun from the waistband of his jeans and handed it back to her. "Just in case," he said, as she took it from him. "Do you still have the money and passport?"

"Yes," she said, patting her back pocket.

Taking the chink of Moonbeam from his pocket, he placed it in the palm of his open hand. The earing pulsated blue, then white, then blue again. Away from the humans and having already turned into the monster, Thaddeus risked wearing it in his ear again.

"Come on," he said, leading Winnie deeper into the wood.

Thaddeus glanced back just once at the abandoned police car. He touched the earing with his fingertips, knowing that he would need all the protection the tiny piece of stone could give him. Because once those searching for him found the dead police officer ripped to pieces in the boot of the car, they wouldn't stop their search until Thaddeus and Winnie were both dead.

Chapter Eight

Lance Stoke and Becka Horton had found a motel just in time. Just before Stoke's skin had begun to more than just prickle, but begin to blister. With a feverish sweat breaking out across his pale brow, he had snatched the key from the young woman behind reception and headed straight for his room and the seclusion he knew it would offer him. Becka had been looking somewhat confused as she stood in the lobby of the rundown motel and watched her inspector hurry away. *What was wrong with him?* she wondered, snatching up her own key and heading toward her room. But today at least she was grateful that Stoke hadn't made some half-cocked attempt at trying to entice her into his room. But she knew at some point she would have to give in to his advances if she was going to get to a place where he was vulnerable enough for her to kill him. Slipping the key into the lock of the hotel door, she knew that he would only continue to slow her down. She knew the nightshifts they had been working were long and tiring and Stoke, like all humans, would need to sleep, but she wasn't human. Becka didn't need to rest her body like Stoke did. She could have continued to search all day and all night long for Blake and the girl if she needed to. And she did need to – if she were going to get to Blake before the authorities – before Stoke did.

Closing the door behind her, Becka pulled her clothes free and let them slide to the floor. She pulled the curtains over the window, throwing her motel room into darkness. It was then that she changed into her true self.

Stoke sat up in bed. He glanced immediately to the right. He could see just the faintest rays of washed-out daylight creeping around the edges of the curtains. Realising that he had slept all day and it would soon be full dark again, he climbed from the bed. That spike of hunger he always felt in the pit of his stomach twisted like a blunt knife scraping against his innards. Although he felt refreshed, it was the thirst – that constant aching for blood – which told him he would need human blood again, and soon. Turning on the shower, he stepped beneath the hot water and let it beat against his muscular back and chest. He hung his head and let the water wash over him. With his thirst burning the back of his throat, his thoughts turned not to Blake, but to his partner, Becka Horton. If he could turn her – make her like him – then he wouldn't have to skulk about, feeding when her back was turned like he had fed on the police officer on the roadside. That seemed like hours ago to him now. Why hadn't he saved himself a pocketful of flesh? He cursed himself, stepping from beneath the water and snatching up the towel. Okay so it would be cold and have the texture of raw jelly, but it would have seen him through. Got him to that point where he found warm flesh. Towelling himself dry, he knew that he would have to catch Blake soon and return to the Carpathian Mountains where he could feed freely or turn Becka. He didn't know which would happen first, and if he was being honest with himself, he relished the thought of both equally.

A knock at his hotel door broke his train of thought. With towel fixed about his waist and his shoulder length blond hair still damp from the shower, he went to the door. Pressing his eye to the spyhole, he stared out into the corridor. Becka stood outside. Unlocking the door, he opened it. He couldn't help but notice how she glanced at his naked chest, then quickly down at the part of him that was covered by the towel. Stoke smiled inwardly at this.

She regained her composure quickly, and looked up into his face. He liked the way her bright hazel eyes matched his stare. He liked the way her black hair tumbled over her shoulders and how her pink lips had a pearly quality to them. And he couldn't help but wonder, like he so often had, what it would feel like to kiss those lips and to be kissed by them.

"Sorry, I didn't mean to disturb you, guv," she said, her pale cheeks suddenly flushing as pink as her lips. "It's just that I've had a call from control. They said they've been trying to reach you."

"I'm a deep sleeper," Stoke half-smiled back at her. "Have they found Blake?"

Becka shook her head. "No, but they've found the police car he stole. And it isn't good."

"And the officers?" Stoke asked, although he knew already what Becka was going to tell him.

"Dead," she said. "Both of them. One was found nearby to where we found that radio out on the road, and the other is in the back of the police car. Both have been ripped to pieces."

Stoke thought of the officer he had killed by the roadside and his stomach almost seemed to jack-knife with thirst again. But Blake had killed the second cop, Stoke thought to himself. Just like Blake killed the couple at the farmhouse. Why leave such a trail of dead bodies? It was like he wanted to be caught.

"I think we should get going, don't you?" Becka said, nudging her inspector into action.

"Sure," Stoke said, glancing into the room, then back at her. "Do you want to come in and wait while I get changed...?"

"No, you're all right, guv," Becka said, stepping away from the door. "I'll wait for you in the car."

Before he'd had a chance to call her back or say anything else, Becka was heading away down the narrow corridor. He watched her go, until she had turned the corner and her trim little figure was out of sight. Stoke closed the door, shutting himself in darkness once again and got dressed.

They sat in silence as Becka drove them out to the woods where a gamekeeper had stumbled across the abandoned police car and the dead cop. Becka had asked Stoke if he'd wanted to go checkout the dead cop on the side of the road first, but Stoke didn't see the point in that. He knew how that cop had died and who had eaten most of him. He stifled a belch at the thought of how good the cop's tongue had tasted. Stoke knew he could have kept up the pretence and gone and had a peek at the dead cop he had killed, but that would've been more time wasted – more distance Blake was putting between them.

A police car was parked next to the entrance to the narrow lane, emergency lights flashing, which led into the woods where Thaddeus and Winnie had spent the night asleep huddled together on the backseat while the cop cried out that he couldn't breathe. Stoke pressed his police badge to the window and the cop on guard waved them through, giving a brisk nod of his head. Becka couldn't help but notice the grim look the cop wore on his face. Two of his colleagues butchered in one night. Even she could understand how that might feel. She had lost too during her long life.

The car rocked and rolled to the left and right as Becka steered the car over the uneven track, heading deeper and deeper into the woods. Both Stoke and Becka could see torchlight weaving and bobbing amongst the trees ahead.

"Okay, stop right here," Stoke said, releasing his seatbelt.

Becka brought the car to a standstill and both got out. They headed through the trees in the direction of the torchlight. As they drew closer they could hear the garbled messages cracking and hissing from hand radios. Then, just ahead and partially covered by broken branches and leaves, was the abandoned police car. With badges in hand, they identified themselves to the three uniformed officers guarding the car.

"So what have we got?" Becka asked one of them.

"PC Crispin…" the officer started to mumble as if searching for the right words.

"Come on, lad, out with it, we haven't got all bloody night," Stoke barked at him.

"Sorry, sir," the cop said, looking somewhat ashamed. "PC Crispin… his body is in the boot of the car."

"Well, what we waiting for?" Stoke said, heading toward the back of the car. "Open it up so we can take a look."

Becka followed, pushing and pulling aside twigs and branches that snagged at her coat and trousers. Aiming his torch at the boot of the car, the officer popped it open. The sight inside was grotesque, and even though both Stoke and Horton had killed many times before, the sight of the dead cop – or what was left of him – was brutal even by their own standards.

"Jeez," Stoke whistled through his front teeth. "Blake didn't leave much behind this time."

"You think Blake did this?" the young cop said, looking away, the sight too much for him to bear – a sight that would haunt him so much that he would take his own life in a few short weeks' time.

"Well I doubt it was the fucking tooth fairy," Stoke said, bending at the knees and peering into the dead cop's open chest cavity. He couldn't help but notice the corpse's heart still remained. Blake had left that much behind at least. The sight of the raw flesh and blood glimmering wetly in the torchlight made Stoke's stomach lurch and his head feel dizzy with thirst.

Standing straight again, he looked at three uniformed officers and said, "Well don't just stand there with your thumbs sticking up your arse, go get the circus rolling. We're going to need Soco..."

"We've already requested them, sir," one of the other cops cut in.

"Well start having a look about... see what you can find," Stoke glared. "Have the next of kin been notified?"

The cop shook his head.

"Well, go get it sorted," Stoke ordered.

The three cops turned away, desperately trying to look busy – as if they knew what to do next, when in truth they were all stunned – grieving for their colleague who lay torn to shreds in the back of the police car.

Turning to look at Becka, Stoke said, "Go see if you can find some tracks. Anything that might suggest which direction Blake and the girl headed. They must have gone on foot, so they might not have gotten very far."

"Yes, guv," Becka said, taking her own torch from her coat pocket – not that she needed it to see in the dark – and headed deeper into the woods. But it wasn't the broken twigs and disturbed foliage that told Becka the direction Blake had headed off in – it was his smell. It was the wolf scent he had left behind.

With Becka now heading off into the woods, and the other cops desperately trying to make themselves look busy, Stoke reached once more into the boot of the car. Looking back just once more to make sure that he wasn't being watched, Stoke slid his hand into the cop's open chest and plucked out his heart. With his fist wrapped around it, Stoke tucked it into his pocket concealed inside his coat. The pocket with the latex gloves and butcher's apron. Bent over the rear of the car and unseen by the other officers, Stoke closed his eyes and slowly licked the blood from his fingers. At once the burning sensation in the back of his throat began to ease and his stomach unknot.

"Guv," Becka said from behind him.

Licking the last of the blood from his lips, Stoke stood up straight and glanced back over his shoulder at her. "Yes?"

"I've found some tracks leading off in this direction," she said.

Together, they set off into the woods. They hadn't gone very far, when Stoke stopped short. Through the darkness he could see the direction in which Blake and the girl had headed. He knew that Blake was close – within his grasp. The hunt was almost over. Becka could smell the wolf and thought the same. Both feared that the other would slow them down. Both knew that if they were to capture Blake they would have to change into their true supernatural selves. But both equally knew that they couldn't strike now. They were too close to the other cops who were still by the abandoned police car.

Turning to look at Becka through the darkness as she stood just feet away, torch in hand, Stoke said, "Horton, head back to the car."

"Why?" She frowned back at him.

"Take the car and head to the other side of the woods. These trees must come to an end. There must be a road. If you leave now we can still head Blake off," Stoke explained.

Staring at him, she knew that if Stoke were to capture Blake first then he would be taken into police custody, and she didn't want that. That wasn't part of her plan. But how could she object without killing Stoke now? She knew that Stoke had no idea what or who Thaddeus Blake truly was. She'd watched Stoke since the fire at Blake's mansion stumble blindly in his off-hand and cocksure manner with no idea that Blake was a werewolf.

Stoke still believed that he was on the hunt for some deranged poet – not the last of the lycanthrope.

"But..." she started.

"Don't argue, sergeant," Stoke said, pulling rank. "Go back to the car and head to the other side of the woods. Between us, we should have Blake trapped."

Looking at the inspector through the darkness, she knew that Stoke would be slower on foot. He wouldn't catch up with Blake however hard he tried. But she just might if she was in the car. Perhaps Stoke had unwittingly helped her.

So with a shrug of her shoulders, she turned away. "You're the guv, guv," she said. "If that's what you want, then I'll see you on the other side of the woods."

For the second time that night, Stoke watched Becka head away from him, and again he watched her as if unable to take his eyes off her until she was out of sight. Once she had gone, Stoke reached inside his coat pocket. Raising PC Crispin's heart to his lips like a bright red apple, Stoke took a bite. With blood splashing onto his chin, he turned and set off at speed in the direction Blake and Winnie were heading.

Chapter Nine

Together – hand in hand – they raced through the woods. Winnie glanced at Thad, then front again as they leapt over a fallen tree trunk. Winnie couldn't help but notice how she had changed. Not purely in appearance, but in strength and agility, too. Although she doubted she was a true vampire yet, she was getting closer to that final metamorphosis. The bloody strips that Thaddeus had been bringing her each night had been sedating that hunger deep inside her and the thirst that raged in the back of her throat. For the first time that she could remember, Winnie felt free, although she knew for the rest of eternity she would be trapped by the night – in darkness. She glanced at Thad again and she couldn't help but think he looked beautiful, with his dark brown hair billowing back from his rugged face, eyes fierce and bright, his strong and powerful claws wrapped about her own. At a startling pace, they raced forward amongst the trees and over the leaf-covered ground. Ahead of them they could see what looked like orange light penetrating the darkness. Streetlights, Thaddeus wondered. Were they close to a road? Near to a town. Someplace they could find transport to keep them heading north. Toward Scotland and the Moonshine he sought there.

Turning his head, Thaddeus looked at Winnie as she sped along beside him. Her now jet black hair streaming out behind her like silk ribbons. Her face as pale as the moon, eyes a neon blue and thick lips blood red. Thaddeus couldn't help but remember how he and Frances had once run, trying to put as much distance between themselves and Nate Varna who hunted them.

Sensing that they might just get to Scotland and the Moonshine before being caught, Thaddeus welcomed the sight of the road he could now see through the trees ahead. Smiling sideways at Winnie through the dark, he said, "Winnie..."

Before he could tell her for the second time that night that she looked beautiful, Thaddeus was struck from behind. Air exploded from his lungs as he staggered forward, losing his grip on Winnie's hand. Without any warning, Winnie was forced backwards through the air, colliding with the nearest tree. Crying out through shock more than pain, Winnie dropped to the ground in a heap. Raking the hair from in front of her eyes, she glanced up to see Thaddeus stooped forward, upper lip rolled back to reveal his jagged teeth. With his claws up, he threw back his head and howled as if readying himself for attack. And just like he had at his mansion, Thaddeus looked more wolf now than man. Pulling herself to her feet, dead leaves falling from her coat and seat of her jeans, Winnie saw who and what had attacked them. A man stepped from the dark. He was tall and lean, his face so very pale it looked like the moon. His eyes shone red, two long fangs jutting from the corners of his mouth. The man's hair was dark blonde and hung over the collar of his coat. His hands were bone white, each finger long like a well sharpened pencil. Without realising she was doing it, Winnie ran the tip of her tongue over the pointed tip of each of her fangs. She felt a sudden heightened sense of awareness, like every nerve ending in her body had been set alight. For someone who was in that place that Thaddeus spoke of – between life and death – she couldn't recall ever feeling so alive. Standing by the tree she had clattered into, Winnie watched this man – this *vampire* – spring through the air at Thaddeus. Thaddeus was just as quick and was throwing himself forward on his muscular haunches. They collided mid-air, their claws glinting like knives as they tore and racked at each other. Thaddeus snarled and howled as he fought with the vampire. They grabbled at each other, Thaddeus driving the vampire back with one powerful swipe of his claws. The thin, pale man flew backwards; his coattails flapping like wings in the dark. The tree shook violently as the man smashed into it. The sound of breaking, snapping branches and splintering bark filled the air.

Thaddeus snapped his head around in a desperate search of Winnie. He needed to know that she was okay – that she hadn't been hurt. Spying her sheltering beneath a nearby tree, he roared, "Run, Winnie! *Run!*"

"No!" she yelled back, rushing forward, claws out and fangs bared. "I won't leave you."

But fearing that Winnie was still yet to fully change and therefore might yet be seduced by Stoke or one of his kind, he shouted, *"Go! Go! Go! Get as far away from here as you can. Run, Winnie!"*

Springing to his feet, a smile dancing over his lips, Stoke could sense Thaddeus's fear for the girl. He looked at her and his smile broadened. She was like him – but perhaps not quite yet. *So beautiful,* he thought. *So virginal.* Reaching out with a hand so smooth it looked like marble in the pale moonlight shining through the leaves above, Stoke said to Winnie, "Don't listen to the wolf. He will kill you just like he's killed every other woman who has loved him." He fixed Winnie with his bright red stare. "You know what I say to be true. You're not like him. You're like me – a vampire. Only a vampire can show you the true blessing of eternal life."

"Don't listen to him, Winnie!" Thad shouted at her. "It's not eternal life that he offers you, but eternal despair."

"Oh, Thaddeus Blake – you lack such imagination." Stoke grinned at him. "That was always the problem with your race. Nothing more than a pack of wild, dumb-minded animals."

Doing his best to ignore Stoke's taunts, Thaddeus looked straight into Winnie's eyes. She looked back, their eyes locked. "Do you trust me, Winnie?"

"Yes," she whispered.

"Then run," Thad said.

Turning on her heels, Winnie ran as Thaddeus threw himself at Stoke again.

With the sound of howling, clawing, and spitting ringing in her ears, Winnie reached a small clearing. Not sure in which direction to run, she stopped and looked back to see Thaddeus break free of the vampire and go bounding away deeper and deeper into the woods. The vampire wasted no time in going after him.

Chapter Ten

With the driver's window wound down, Becka Horton thought at first the sound of howling she could hear was that of the wind and not a giant wolf. Pressing the sole of her boot hard against the brake, the car skidded to a stop on the desolate country road. The wood loomed tall on her left like a city made of trees. To her right lay bleak and barren moorland. It just looked dark and flat, like a giant bottle of black ink had been tipped over, its contents free to gush away for as far as the eye could see. The howling came again, this time deep and throaty. Becka knew it to be the unmistakeable howl of a werewolf. Yanking hard on the car door, she forced it open with such force that she nearly spilled onto the road. Blake was near and she wanted him. She wanted to reach him before Stoke. Never again would she let Blake get away from her. With her hair bouncing about her shoulders, Becka fled into the woods in search of the werewolf she had spent much of her life hunting. Head tilted back, she sniffed at the air, searching out the wolf's scent. Any whiff of it would be good. But there was none. She headed deeper and deeper into the wood, moving faster and faster, gathering speed, mindful not to change just in case…

Stopping suddenly, chest rising and falling as she drew breath, Becka spied movement ahead. She could see someone running toward her through the darkness. It wasn't Thaddeus. She would have smelt him by now. The figure was too short – too slender. It was the girl. This Winter McCall that Blake had been traveling with. Slinking back into the shadows, Becka waited – letting the girl draw nearer before stepping out from behind a tree and into her path. Stopping short, then staggering backwards at the sudden appearance of the pretty young woman, Winnie let out a scream. Winnie had no idea who the woman was or where she had come from. She was sure she'd never seen her before. But Becka knew who and *what* Winnie was. She could see that the girl was a vampire. Her bright gleaming blue eyes and sleek jet black hair told Becka that. Knowing that she was just feet from Thaddeus's companion – his new love – Becka realised that to capture her would entice Blake out.

So smiling, Becka looked at Winnie and said, "Hello."

Staring back, and with a half-smile, Winnie said, "Do I know you?"

Stoke's claws passed inches from Thaddeus's throat as they continued to rip and tear at each other. Leaves sprayed up all around them as if they had been consumed by a whirlwind.

"Why don't you just die!" Stoke grimaced as he shot forward again, claws like daggers.

"You first," Thad snarled, raking his claw down the length of the vampire's face. The skin shredded in five jagged lines. But no sooner had the flesh split open, it was healing again, as if being stitched up by an invisible needle and thread.

"I will take your head back to Nicodemus," Stoke warned, leaping through the air in one quick bound and landing behind Thad.

Thad spun around to face his enemy once again. "Frances didn't die like you think she did," he tried to reason with him.

"You bit her, didn't you?" Stoke hissed, coming forward, his claws raking at Thaddeus's throat again, just wanting to rip his head clean off.

Thad ducked, rolling away in a whirl of claws and hair. "I loved Frances," he said, springing back at Stoke.

"It didn't take you long to fall in love with another," Stoke sneered, lurching back and away from Thaddeus once more. "*Another* vampire. I don't believe you love that girl any more than you really loved Frances."

"I don't care what you believe!" Thad roared at him, both locked again as they fought with one another.

"You take female vampires as brides so as to use them as nothing more than shields. You think we won't come after you because you love one of our kind. That might have been true when you shared your life with Frances, but not now, wolf. That girl might look like Frances, but it isn't her. Nothing can save you this time."

"Just leave me in peace!" Thad roared, striking out at Stoke once more. But before his claws had made yet another set of ragged tracks in the vampire's face, Stoke had flipped backwards and out of reach.

Instead of landing with poise and grace like he had so many times before, he lurched and wobbled as if the ground was unstable somehow. Stoke looked down at his booted feet that were now fast sinking in what looked like a quagmire. The earth almost seemed to bubble up and shift as Stoke began to sink into it. As if realising his fate, Stoke tried to lift his right foot, then left out of the bog he had fallen into. But the more he tried to wade forward, back to solid ground where Thaddeus stood and watched, the quicker he sank beneath the ground. It was like he was being swallowed up.

He looked at Thaddeus who was just out of reach. He knew he would get no help from him. Stoke glanced up, but the overhanging branches were too far out of reach. He looked back at Thaddeus, who stood watching, giant claws swinging by his sides, shirt and coat torn and bloodied from his fight with Stoke.

The mud was up to his waist now and he could feel it growing tighter about his thighs as it continued to pull him under.

"Help me – get me out of here…" he asked Thaddeus.

"Never," Thaddeus said, a grim look pulled down over his face.

The mud bubbled up around Stoke's chest. He raised his arms looking like a drowning man. "If you save me, then I'll save you. I'll stop chasing you."

"You lie," Thaddeus said, wiping blood from his claws. "You won't stop hunting me until you have my head to take back to your king, and I won't stop running until all of the vampires are dead."

"I knew it," Stoke said with one last devilish grin.

"Knew what?" Thad asked, watching the mud swell up around Stoke's shoulders.

"You don't love that girl," Stoke said, tilting his head back as the thick mud now lapped about his neck.

Thad stared at the pale face that now watched him from the mud. "I do love her."

"You just said that you won't stop until you've killed all vampires," Stoke gasped, sucking down a throat full of air. "She is a vampire."

A scream broke the silence that now hung over the bog. Thad looked back over his shoulder now fearing for Winnie. Had Stoke come alone? Of course he hadn't. Thad remembered that he had seen two people approach the farmhouse where he had hidden with Winnie. Stoke began to chuckle – or was that gargle? Thad couldn't be sure as he looked back at the bog to see the mud slosh up over Stoke's chin and into his mouth. He wanted to stay and watch – to really make sure that Stoke was dead. But the scream – it rang in his ears over and over. He knew that Winnie was in danger. He looked once more down at Stoke, just his nose and eyes staring out of the mud. Convinced that Stoke had no way of saving himself, Thaddeus turned and raced away from the bog in search of Winnie.

Chapter Eleven

Taking a step closer to Winnie, Sergeant Becka Horton took her police badge from her coat pocket with one hand, concealing the other behind her back. The fingers on the hand that she had concealed became elongated as if stretched somehow. From each fingertip protruded a hooked claw. She could see uncertainty – smell the fear – leaking from the girl. Becka could sense that the girl had not fully turned, and therefore was not in full control of her powers – her full strength. Becka knew that killing the girl Blake travelled with would be easier than she had first thought. Becka's heart raced as she stepped closer to Winnie through the darkness.

"You have nothing to fear," Becka smiled, her fistful of blades still hidden from view. She held her badge up for Winnie to see. "I'm a police officer."

Winnie looked down at the gleaming badge and as she did, Becka whipped out her claw-like hand from behind her back. Before Winnie had a chance to see it and the danger she was in, Becka was thrown back through the air and away from her. She screamed and Winnie looked up to see a flash of red race by.

"Ruby?" Winnie gasped, seeing her friend standing at the foot of a nearby tree where the police officer now lay in a crumpled heap. And just like before, Winnie could see that her friend had her hood pulled up as if to hide her face. Winnie felt grateful for this. She wasn't sure that she could look upon that maggot-infested face again.

Rolling onto her side feeling dazed and confused, Becka looked up to see who or what had suddenly thrown her clear of Winnie. With eyes half open and the back of her skull feeling as if it had had a sledgehammer buried in it, she looked up at the figure in the red hooded coat who stood just feet way. Before unconsciousness took her, Becka couldn't help but think that the figure standing in the middle of the wood looked something close to Little Red Riding Hood setting off to see her grandmother – the big, bad wolf.

With her hood still pulled up, the sides of it covering her decaying face in shadow, Ruby Little approached her friend again. "You should run, Winnie." Her voice floated like a whisper from beneath her hood. Winnie tried desperately not to picture the maggots writhing beneath it, squirming out of her friend's nostrils and the cracks in her broken flesh.

"Ruby?" Winnie said, taking a tender step toward her dead friend.

Ruby threw back the hood, her face sickly-green in colour. Her skull shining white through the last remaining lumps of flesh stuck to it. There wasn't even enough for the maggots to feast on. Her eye sockets were just two deep wells of darkness. *"Run, Winnie!"* But this time Ruby's voice was far more than a whisper. It was an ear-piercing scream.

Gasping for breath, Winnie ran and ran. Tree branches clawed at her clothes, hair, and flesh as if wanting to hold her back, to keep her prisoner in the wood. She slapped them aside like hands reaching for her as she raced onward. Looking up, Winnie saw the road again. It was like a winding snake on the other side of the treeline. With clouds of hot breath escaping her mouth, Winnie sprang from the wood and onto the road as if being shot from a cannon. Landing on her feet, Winnie straightened up, hair blowing about her face and shoulders. A claw gripped her arm and she screamed. But before the sound of her fear fully escaped her throat, a claw clamped down over her mouth.

"Shhh," Thaddeus breathed in her ear.

Turning, Winnie fell into Thaddeus's arms. She smelt the blood covering his clothes and skin. And her first thought wasn't that he might be injured, but of her growing hunger. She held him tight, pulling him close, soaking up that smell of fresh blood.

"Are you okay?" she whispered into his ear.

"I'll live," he said, easing her out of his arms.

"And the vampire?" she asked.

"Dead," he said, taking her hand in his and shuffling away up the road.

Winnie looked at his leg. There was a jagged tear in his jeans along the length of his right thigh. The denim was soaked black with blood. "You are injured," she breathed, placing one arm about his broad shoulders and helping him along.

"Are you okay?" he asked, brushing aside her concern for him.

"I'm fine," Winnie said, looking back over her shoulder in the direction she had come. She could see no sign of Ruby. "There was a cop in those woods. A young woman."

"That's why we have to keep moving," Thad said, wincing in pain and moving forward with Winnie's help. "That cop was probably a vampire too."

Without warning, he stopped dead.

"What's wrong?" Winnie asked, feeling suddenly exposed on the road, but not wanting to go back into the wood either.

"What's that noise?" he whispered.

Cocking her head to one side, Winnie listened. There was a deep rumbling in the distance, but it was getting steadily closer. "Thunder?"

"No, it's not thunder," Thaddeus said with a shake of his head. He looked into the distance. He could see a bridge. "It's a train. C'mon."

Gripping her hand in his, Thaddeus limped as fast as he could up the centre of the road and toward the railway bridge. With each step he took, he made a grunting noise in the back of his throat. The sound of the approaching train grew louder and Thaddeus and Winnie moved along the road toward it.

Chapter Twelve

Becka heard the sound of her name being called. It sounded weak and far off, as if coming from another world. Her head still hurt and she just wanted the sound of the voice to go away. It was irritating.

"Horton," the voice came again. "Becka, help me!"

With long eyelashes fluttering, Becka half opened her eyes and peered about. She was still on the ground at the base of the tree. The figure in the red coat had gone. Had she really been there at all? Becka wondered, dragging herself into an upright position amongst the leaves and dirt covering the floor of the wood. But something had pushed her – thrown her – across the clearing and into the tree. It was like the red hooded figure had wanted to protect Winnie.

"Becka," the voice came again. It sounded muffled and weak, like whoever was calling her name was choking on something.

Using the tree as some kind of prop, Becka forced herself to her feet, the back of her head still feeling as if it had been caved in. She touched the painful patch with her fingertips, then inspected them in the moonlight. She couldn't see any signs of blood.

"Help me! Pleeeease!" the voice cried out, sounding scratchy and broken.

Cocking her head to the right and listening intently, Becka thought the voice sounded like that of Stoke. "Guv?" she called out, stepping away from the tree and heading in the direction of the voice.

Horton hadn't gone very far when she saw what looked like a small crescent shaped moon staring out of a boggy area of ground ahead of her. The mud around the white moon bubbled up and popped. It shifted and writhed. The moon disappeared then resurfaced. It spoke.

"Beck..." then it was gone again.

"Guv?" Horton breathed, running toward the bog. She stopped abruptly. Becka suspected that Stoke had stumbled into the bog as he'd made his way blindly through the woods in search of Blake and the girl. Saving him now would only slow her down again. Blake and the girl were getting away again, and she knew this was the closest she had got to him in all the years she had hunted the wolf. Stoke's face partially appeared again. She caught sight of his eyes as they locked with hers. For the first time ever she saw fear in them. Gone was his arrogance – cockiness. Becka knew she should let him die – she intended on killing him anyway so this would save her the job. But part of her wondered whether this was the right time to let Stoke die. Her senses told her not. Was it the sight of the figure in the red hood that had spooked her? Becka wasn't sure.

"Help," Stoke rasped before disappearing again.

"Oh, shit," Becka muttered, fearing that she might regret the decision she was about to make. Reaching up, she took hold of one of the tree branches that swayed in the wind above her head. Turning her fist into a claw, she yanked a branch free of the tree with ease. Kneeling at the edge of the bog, she lowered the huge branch out over the bog then drove the end of it down into the mud where she had last seen Stoke resurface.

"Grab the branch," she hollered at the top of her voice. "Guvnor, take hold of it and I'll drag you out."

She felt the end of the branch move beneath the mud, like it had become heavier somehow. Hoping that Stoke had grabbed hold of the branch beneath the mud, she began to yank backwards on it. The bog began to ripple at its centre like a thick, black wave coming slowly toward the shore. Gritting her teeth and leaning back, she pulled again. Squinting, she looked back at the bog and could see the crown of Stoke's head, and then his face appear from beneath the mud. Leaning back further still, she yanked on the branch, her hands still claws to give her further grip. She hoped that in the gloom of the woods, Stoke wouldn't see them. He'd missed a great big fucking bog after all, she thought to herself.

Becka looked back at the bog once more as she heaved and heaved. Stoke's head and shoulders were now free of the mud that stuck to him like tar. Sensing now that he was out of danger, Becka let her hands change back to their human form once more. With Stoke now within reach of her, Becka let go of the branch and held out her hands. Taking hold of them with his own, Stoke clung to her as she pulled him free of the bog. Both collapsed onto to their backs, both panting and drawing breath.

"Thanks," he gasped, rolling onto his side and spitting mud and grit from his mouth.

"How did you get so deep into the woods and so quick?" Becka asked, pulling herself up into a sitting position.

"The only thing I got deep in was that shit," he coughed and spluttered, hooking his thumb in the direction of the bog.

Becka let the fact that he had reached the furthest reaches of the wood on foot in the time it had taken her to drive go for now and said, "Well, it looks as if Blake got away from us again. Did you see him?"

"No," Stoke said, hooking crusty scabs of mud from his nostrils and ears and flicking it away. "I stumbled into the bog in the dark." He clawed clumps of mud from his face and hair. It was caked to his coat, trousers, and boots.

"We'd better get going," Becka said, standing up, keen to get after Blake again now that she was so close.

"He won't get far, Stoke said, slowly opening his hand and staring down at his grubby palm. What looked like a small diamond earring sat in his hand. It almost seemed to pulse blue with light.

"What's that?" Becka asked, drawing a sharp intake of breath at the sight of it. She knew exactly what that small chip of blue stone was. Horton had seen it before. It was a piece of the Moonbeam.

"Dunno," Stoke shrugged, seemingly unable to take his eyes off it.

"Where did you get it?" Becka whispered, watching how the Moonbeam pulsed like a heartbeat in the palm of Stoke's grubby hand. She had to stifle the urge to lunge for it. Take it for herself.

"I found it," Stoke said, remembering how he had snatched it from Blake's ear as they had fought. Then slowly curling his fingers around it, Stoke stood up, placing the shard of Moonbeam into his trouser pocket and out of sight, knowing there was no place Blake could now hide from him. "We should find someplace to rest. Perhaps back at the motel we stayed at last night. It isn't far."

"But what about Blake?" Becka said. "We have to get after him."

"What? Like this?" he said, flapping the tails of his mud-soaked coat at her. "I need to freshen up."

Becka couldn't help but notice that arrogant tone was back in his voice again despite being saved by her. Why hadn't she let the prick die? She briefly wondered. But then she knew she had done the right thing by saving him. If she had let him sink to the bottom of that filthy quagmire, that piece of Moonbeam would have been lost forever. She would need to get it off Stoke. Then once she had it, she would kill him once and for all.

"Where did you leave the car?" Stoke asked, striding away in his muddy clothes.

"On the road," Becka said, pointing him in the right direction.

As she walked silently beside him, Stoke shot her a sideways glance. He knew now that he had the Moonbeam, he could track Blake without hindrance. There was no need for him to keep up the pretence of being a dutiful police officer. There was now no need for him to be held back by his partner, Sergeant Horton. Back at the motel, she would either become like him or die. He didn't really care for her anymore. Not after setting eyes on Winnie. She had been the most beautiful vampire he had ever seen. Yes, she looked like the legendary Frances, but Winnie was somehow more beautiful. There was an innocence about her. Stoke liked that. He would like to be the one to take that innocence away. He followed Becka through the wood and out on to the road where she had left the car. As he watched her climb inside, he decided that back at the motel he would simply take her, then kill her. There was no need to make her like him. He had decided who he wanted his new bride to be, and once he had killed Blake, he would be able to take the girl as his own.

Becka watched Stoke slide into the passenger seat. She glanced down at the pocket where that piece of Moonbeam now lay hidden and knew that Stoke had no idea what it was that he had found – what Blake must have dropped while escaping through the wood. Horton couldn't wait to now finally kill Stoke and take back that piece of Moonbeam.

Starting up the car, she sped them both back in the direction of the motel.

Chapter Thirteen

With her arm still around Thad's shoulder, Winnie helped him down the embankment at the side of the railway line. The rough ballast made a clacking sound as both lost their footing and they slid down into the cess running parallel with the tracks. Thad made a grunting sound deep in the back of his throat and gripped his thigh, which was still bleeding. Winnie looked away. The sight of the blood streaming darkly through the rip in his jeans made her stomach somersault with hunger.

"Are you okay?" she asked, still facing away from him and looking along the tracks. She could see a small railway station in the distance. There was a train at the platform.

"I'll heal soon enough," Thad said, pulling himself to his feet. He knew why she was looking away, and he put one hand to a cut that bled around the curve of his jaw. The blood felt tacky there where it had started to congeal already.

"I can see a train," Winnie said, pointing down the tracks.

"Let's see if we can't get on board," he said, taking her hand in his and hobbling away toward it.

Winnie trotted beside him, the smell of blood almost intoxicating now. She tilted her head back and breathed deeply, trying to take in as much of the cold night air as possible. Anything to dilute the growing scent of his blood and her hunger for it.

Reaching the station, they ran up a short ramp and onto the platform. It was deserted, apart from the mail train that sat in the station, engine purring like a giant cat and belching black clouds of diesel smoke up into the night. Slowly the train started to pull out of the station. Thad tried to run faster, but every time he put his foot to the ground a sudden explosion of pain jolted up the length of his leg. Hands still gripped tight, Winnie and Thad ran alongside it as it quickly gathered speed. Reaching out, Winnie took hold of one of the large doors and slid it back. The door squealed and shuddered on its unoiled tracks. Gritting his teeth and forcing himself to run faster, Thad pushed Winnie toward the opening inside of the vast carriage.

"Get in!" he yelled over the roar of the engine.

Springing into the air, Winnie lept inside the train. With hair flying out behind her, she leant out, gripped Thaddeus's wrist and heaved him inside. She yanked the door shut as the train lurched over a set of points as it cleared the station and headed north into the night. Pin-wheeling her arms, Winnie fell backwards onto Thad, who lay on a heap of mailbags that covered the carriage floor. He growled in pain as she unintentionally struck his injured leg.

"Sorry," she gasped, rolling over on top of him.

Now that her face was no more than an inch from Thaddeus's, the waft of fresh blood leaking from a gash beneath his jawline was overwhelming. Closing her eyes, she lowered her head, pressing her soft lips over the cut. With her fangs out and blissfully unaware of what she was doing, she punctured the skin around the cut just beneath Thaddeus's jaw. Winnie felt a warm gush of his blood fill her mouth, and at once the burning sensation in the back of her throat eased. The knot in her stomach began to untie itself as it soaked up the blood that was now gushing down Winnie's throat. Holding her close to him, Thaddeus tilted back his head and let her feed from him. He knew what was happening wasn't ideal, but there was no other way he could get food for Winnie. Not until they were off the train. How long until that would be he didn't know, but he knew that if Winnie didn't feed, she would fail to complete her change and die.

When he too started to feel lightheaded, he knew that he would have to pull back – stop Winnie from feeding from him. He had given his blood to Frances on very rare occasions, when there was no other choice available to them. But it was nothing more than a quick fix. Lycanthrope blood wasn't like that of a human's or any other type of living creature. He could remember Frances describing it once like the difference between real coffee and the decaffeinated blend. It kind of hit the spot, but didn't give you the kick you were really looking for. Knowing that if Winnie drank for too much longer he would pass out, he eased Winnie's mouth from over the cut. With her eyes half shut and lips smeared red with his blood, he kissed her. With a greed and passion she hadn't felt before, Winnie kissed him back. Losing his hands in her thick, dark hair, he felt her hands fumble open the front of his shirt and explore his bare chest. They worked their way downwards, unfastening the belt about his waist. Feeling her cool touch against him, Thaddeus slid his hands from her hair and began pulling free her clothes. Once they were both naked, Thaddeus wrapped his strong arms about her slender frame and lay her down on her back amongst the mail bags. Looking up at him, the taste of his blood still fresh in her mouth, Winnie drew her knees up and pulled Thaddeus down over her.

    As the train lurched and swayed over the tracks, they made love. They moved slowly at first, both suppressing the urgent desire they'd hidden for so long from each other. But as the train raced north, their lovemaking grew stronger and more passionate. Winnie had never felt such an intense sense of love before, and she was happy to give herself to someone for the first time. With arms wrapped tightly about his back, she pulled him over her, holding him tight, never wanting to let go.

    "I love you," she sighed.

    In his heart, Thaddeus knew that he had fallen in love with Winnie too. Was this new love any more intense than the love he had once felt for Revekka or Frances? It had felt different with each of them. Not less. Not more. Just different. But always real.

"I love you, too," he whispered right back, then kissed her all over again.

They lay in each other's arms, the train carriage swaying all about them. With her head rested against Thaddeus's naked chest she could hear the steady thrum of his heart. She closed her eyes. For the first time she could remember – probably ever – Winnie felt loved – complete. As Thaddeus lay, he made small circles over the nape of her neck with his fingertips. Winnie liked the feel of his cool touch and she prayed that the train would never stop. That they would never have to get off. Doing so would break the spell she now felt had been cast over her. But knowing that the train would eventually stop and their journey would be at an end, she whispered, "So what next?"

"Sleep," Thaddeus said.

"I didn't mean that. I meant what's next for us?" Winnie asked.

Slowly working his fingers from the nape of her neck and down the gentle curve of her back, Thaddeus said, "We need to get to that house my father once shared with Karl when they went abroad on their mining trips in search of precious stones. I'm hoping that Karl will know where the Moonshine is."

"What makes you think he will know?" Winnie asked over the clickerty-clack of the train.

"He's a werewolf too, remember?" Thaddeus started to explain. "He got bitten by my aunt while I went in search of my cousin Dominika who had killed Revekka. Karl will know that his life is at risk if the vampires ever learnt that I was not the sole survivor of my race. Out of guilt for what I did to his daughter, I have kept away from him so as not to bring suspicion on him.

Besides, I thought I had drawn a truce with the vampires while I shared my life with Frances. But now that is all over, I have to find the Moonshine. It is the only way of destroying the vampires once and for all. Karl knows that. He has the Moonbeam, so he would have wanted to find the Moonshine just in case he needed to bring them together..."

"But if he had found the Moonshine, wouldn't he have used it already to kill the vampires?" Winnie cut in, propping herself up on one elbow so she could look at Thaddeus.

"No, because he knew that would have killed Frances, too," Thaddeus said. "He might blame me for what happened to his daughter Revekka, but he doesn't hate me. If he did, he would have used the Moonshine."

"That's if he has it," Winnie said thoughtfully.

"Let's hope he does, because I'm all out of ideas," Thaddeus said.

"You told me once that the Moonshine is like some kind of prism, and if the Moonbeam is placed inside it by a wolf, the rays from the Moonbeam will spread out across the world, killing all the vampires," Winnie said, looking at him from beneath her fringe.

"That's right," Thad nodded.

"Then won't those rays of moonlight kill me, too?" she asked softly, trying to hide the fear in her voice.

"Hey," Thad said, reaching out and taking her hands in his. "As long as you're alive, I have no intention of ever using the Moonshine..."

"Then why look for it?" she cut in.

"Because I want another truce," Thad said, looking into her eyes. "I want to tell the vampires hunting us that unless they leave us in peace forevermore, I will use the Moonshine. For once I will have power over them. The Moonshine will bring me freedom at last. It will make us both free, Winnie. We will be able to stop running and have a proper life together."

"So the Moonshine is like some kind of deterrent – a bit like nuclear weapons. You attack us and we attack you?" she asked him.

"Yeah, I guess," he said.

"But if they know you love me, then the vampires will know you will never use the Moonshine, because if they die, I die," Winnie said.

"There is only one vampire who knows what you really are, and he's lying dead at the bottom of some quagmire back in that wood," Thaddeus tried to reassure her. "No one knows that Michelle bit and turned you, Winnie. That is our secret." There was a moment of silence between them before Thaddeus spoke again. "So you never told me how you got away from that cop."

"Cop?" Winnie frowned at the sudden change in topic.

"The one you said you saw in the woods."

"Ruby saved me."

"But's she's dead," Thaddeus reminded her. "Died of a drug overdose beneath the arches..."

"I do remember what happened," Winnie cut in. "How could I ever forget? She was my best friend. I loved her like a sister."

"How long had you known her for?" Thaddeus asked, seeing the sudden flash of hurt in Winnie's eyes. "Did you meet her on the streets?"

"No, we met before that," Winnie started to explain. "I met her in this orphanage the local authority had placed us in. Neither of us were proper orphans. We both had living parents, but both of us had previously run away from the care homes we'd been placed in, so they thought we'd do better – be less likely to escape from the orphanage."

"Escape? You make it sound like a prison," Thad said, watching her pluck up her disregarded shirt and wrap it like a shawl about her shoulders.

"It may as well been a prison," Winnie said. "It was far out of town and set on top of some remote hill. But me and Ruby escaped from time to time. Climbed over the wall without the staff knowing. Once we even went to the cinema together. That was a really fun day. I hadn't known Ruby long, she had been living at the orphanage for about a year before I was sent there. It had been my idea to go over the wall. I'd heard that Daniel Craig was in a new movie. I kinda always thought he was cute, so I suggested that we should go. But it was more than that. I'd only been at the orphanage a few days and I was already beginning to feel like a prisoner."

"So did you escape?" Thad asked, suddenly finding himself curious about Winnie's past life. He had told Winnie so much about himself, but realised he knew very little about her.

"Sure, we escaped," Winnie said with a smile, remembering the time she had shared with her friend Ruby Little.

Part Two

Winnie & Ruby

Chapter Fourteen

I didn't realise how much Ruby disliked going to the movies until that weekend. After some persuasion from me, we went to see *The Girl With The Dragon Tattoo*. The film was rated 18 and neither of us were old enough. I was just fifteen at the time and Ruby had been fourteen. I know some girls can look older than their age, but I don't think either of us did.

We'd climbed over the wall that surrounded the orphanage and followed the road into the nearest town. About a mile out, I started to get the jitters and looked for some excuse to head back without looking like a coward in front of my newfound friend.

"You know, I don't think this is such a good idea," I said to Ruby, who walked beside me, the hood of her red coat pulled up against the wind.

"It was your idea," she reminded me, pulling her hands up into her sleeves. "I don't even like going to the cinema. It's so *boooring!*"

"Perhaps we should head back to the orphanage," I said, slowing down.

"What's the real problem?" Ruby said, peeking out at me from beneath the bright red hood of her coat. "Scared that the staff will notice we've gone missing? Are you scared you'll get into trouble with Mr. Duvall?"

The thought of that creep did cause gooseflesh to break out all over my arms and back, but it wasn't him. "No, it's nothing like that. I just realised we don't have any money."

Smiling, Ruby pulled something from her coat pocket. "I've got a tenner," she said, two crisp five pound notes fluttering between her fingers in the wind.

"Were did you get them?" I asked, open-mouthed. None of the kids at the orphanage had access to any money or any way of earning it as far as I knew.

"I found it," she shrugged, heading back along the road in the direction of town.

I trotted after her. I wasn't sure whether to believe Ruby or not. My first thought was that perhaps she had stolen it from somewhere. "Where did you find it?" I pushed.

"Can't remember," she said and sped up, leaving me standing alone in the centre of the road.

The town wasn't big. It just had the one main road that ran through it. There was a post office, chemist, a supermarket, a fish and chip shop, a library, I think, and a pub. At the end of town was an old theatre which had been converted into a small cinema that showed one or two of the latest movies on the weekend. It was only as we got in line and looked at all the other adults waiting, I realised Ruby and I looked out of place. It wasn't just our shabby clothes and unkempt hair, but we just looked too young.

"I think we should forget this," I said.

"Why?" Ruby asked, as if enjoying my agony somehow.

I leant forward, and cupping my hand around my mouth, I whispered into her ear. "We look way too young. We look like a couple of kids."

"Put this on," Ruby said, reaching into her pocket again and pulling out a lipstick.

"Where did you get that?" I asked.

"The same place I found the money," she said, shoving the lipstick into my hand. "Put it on. It will make you look you older."

"I'm not so sure…" I started.

"Stop being a chicken, Winnie," Ruby nudged me. "It's just a bit of fun."

"But what if I get caught?"

"So what?" she shrugged. "Scared the lipstick police are gonna lock you up?"

"I'm not scared," I told her. Ruby was a couple of years younger than me, but yet seemed older somehow. More daring. Not wanting to look like a coward in front of someone younger than myself, I turned my back on the others in line outside the old theatre and covered my lips with the lipstick. It was bright red and I could feel that some of it had got stuck to my front teeth.

"How do I look?" I asked, positioning my long auburn hair so as to cover the sides of my face.

"Like a movie star," she smiled.

"I meant, how *old* do I look?"

"Twenty-five at least," she said.

"Yeah, right," I groaned. "What about you?"

"What about me?" she asked.

"Aren't you gonna put some on?"

Ruby shook her head, taking back the lipstick and placing it into her pocket. "I could cover myself in that shit and I'd still never be let in to see the film. Besides, if we keep back some of the money, I'll buy you a bag of chips to eat on the way home."

"That place isn't our home," I reminded her.

"It is for now," she said, then quickly added. "Go on, Winnie, everyone is going in."

"What about you?"

"You go and buy a ticket," Ruby explained. "Then once you're inside and before the film starts, go down the fire escape and open the door. I'll be waiting around the back for you. I'll get in to see the dumb movie for free, while you get to drool over Daniel Craig and we get to keep a fiver to buy some chips with later."

Before I'd had the chance to object, Ruby had slipped away into the alleyway that ran alongside the old theatre. With my lips as bright as a fire engine, I queued by myself, feeling ever more anxious as I finally reached the ticket office. I was sweating so much I felt an ice cold bead of sweat run from off my brow and splash onto my cheek like a tear. But the old guy sitting behind the glass ticket booth didn't even look up as he punched me out a ticket and I handed him the money.

Once inside the theatre, I waited until the lights had gone out, then got up and followed the luminous green fire-escape signs until I was in a corridor which ran parallel to the auditorium. I carefully eased open the fire door to find Ruby grinning in the alleyway.

"Nice one, Winnie," she said, squeezing past me.

She hadn't even stepped fully out of the cold when an ear-shattering alarm began to wail.

"What the fuck is that?" Ruby yelled, throwing her hands over her ears.

"I must have tripped the fire alarm when I opened the door," I said, heart beginning to race.

I saw a shadow appear along the corridor wall as someone came running to see what was happening.

"Someone's coming," I hissed, shoving Ruby back out into the cold.

"Hey, you!" I heard someone shout. But I was too scared to look back. Instead I raced out into the alleyway and after Ruby, who was already disappearing back along the High Street. I followed behind and it wasn't long before I was panting and gasping for breath. For someone so little, Ruby could certainly run fast. Ahead I could see the pub. Ruby seemed to slow. Had she run out of breath too? I wondered, a stich now jabbing me in the side. I could see a man come from within the pub. He had a bottle of beer swinging from his fist. He placed it down onto one of the beer tables outside as he lit a cigarette. Then speeding up again,

Ruby raced past the pub, snatching up the bottle of beer as she went.

"Hey!" the man hollered after her.

Without even glancing at him, I raced past in pursuit of Ruby. Perhaps if the guy had been younger, he might have bothered coming after us. But I was way younger and fitter than him, and even I was having trouble catching up with Ruby.

She didn't stop until the town was some way behind us. I trotted after her, that stich now feeling like I was being poked with a hot blade. Ahead, Ruby left the road, darting down a side track. I followed. The track looked well worn, and the grass was faded and yellow in patches. Bushes and brambles stood tall on either side of us. At the end of the path, Ruby stopped. Finally catching up with her and drawing in deep lungfuls of breath, I could see that she had brought me to what looked like a derelict farmhouse. The windows and front door was missing, as was much of the roof.

Ruby looked at me from beneath her hood. She didn't even look like she had broken out in a sweat. She held up the bottle of beer, threw back her head, and took one long gulp. Ruby belched, which was quickly followed by a series of giggles.

"Want some?" she asked, handing me the bottle.

"Thanks," I gasped, still feeling out of breath and now thirsty. I put the bottle to my lips and took a swig. Ice cold beer flooded into my mouth. I didn't care for the taste very much, but it went someway to washing away my aching thirst. I handed the bottle back to Ruby and wiped the red lipstick from my mouth with the sleeve of my threadbare sweater. Ruby drank from the bottle again, then stepped into the dilapidated farmhouse. I followed her inside, covering my nose with my sleeve almost at once. The place stank of stale urine. There were no real rooms as such. The house was one large empty shell. The staircase barely remained. The few remaining steps that were left disappeared up into the darkness. The banister was splintered and the once white paint that had covered it was now grey and flaking away.

"Hold this," Ruby said, shoving the bottle back into my hands.

She went to the foot of the broken staircase. Taking hold of what was left of the banister, Ruby began to climb the stairs and up into the darkness.

"Where are you going?" I asked, feeling fearful for her. Even under her slight frame, I could hear the stairs creaking and could see the bannister wobbling.

"Wait there," she said without looking back.

I watched as Ruby's red coat disappeared up into the darkness. Wasn't she scared? I wondered. I looked about the empty shell of a house and could see that the floor was littered with old beer cans, discarded condoms, black and charred sheets of tin foil, and syringes. How did Ruby even know this place existed?

"Hey, Winnie," she yelled from above. "Watch this!"

"Watch what?" I called back, going to the foot of the stairs.

Ruby suddenly appeared out of the darkness like a giant red bat. She swung down on a length of thick blue rope. Someone had made what looked like a noose at one end and this Ruby clung to as she swung back and forth.

"It's a swing!" she beamed, her hood flying back and revealing her pretty young face. Her long blonde hair snaked out behind her.

She swung back and forth over the large empty space which I guessed had once been a lounge. I had never seen such a wide grin on her face. For the first time, swinging back and forth in that disused house, she looked happy.

"Look, Winnie, I'm flying!" she cried out with excitement. "I'm as free as a bird. I can go anywhere!"

She swung back and forth over my head as I stood and watched her.

"Wanna have a go?" she called down to me, her momentum finally slowing.

"Nah, you're okay, I don't think I'll bother," I said.

"Don't be chicken, Winnie," Ruby laughed, loosening the noose about her wrist and dropping back down on the ancient floorboards. An empty beer can rolled away into a corner of the room.

"It's safe as houses," she said, standing on tiptoe so she could still keep hold of the end of the rope. "Some of the boys from town fixed it up. They come up here and do a bit of weed and stuff. When they're high, they take to the rope. They say it's a right buzz doing the rope when off your face. They say they're flying in more ways than one." She giggled again.

I looked at the rope and then the pit of darkness at the top of the stairs.

"No one's up there," she said as if being able to read my mind. "The lads don't come up here no more. The whole place is going to be built on. Some big outter town supermarket is going up. Go on, have a go, Winnie, before the bleeding place gets pulled down."

Handing her the bottle and swapping it for the rope, I climbed the stairs with the noose wrapped tightly about my fist. The stairs felt more unstable than they looked. They creaked with every careful step I took. As I reached the darkness, I looked back over my shoulder and down at Ruby. She stood looking up at me, taking another gulp from the bottle.

"Go on, Winnie, you'll love it."

Facing front again, I stepped up into the darkness. I could just make out that the other end of the blue rope had been tied about the bannister fixed to the landing. I yanked on the rope as hard as I could. The bannister wobbled, but it felt secure enough.

"C'mon, Winnie," Ruby cheered me on from below.

Closing my eyes and biting onto my lower lip, I gripped the rope as tightly as I could then jumped from the top of the stairs. With my stomach racing up into my throat, I swung out over the empty room below.

"Woo-hoo!" Ruby cried.

I raced back and forth through the air. I dared to open my eyes. I must have looked like freaking Tarzan as I swept backwards and forwards. The banister creaked above me, but I no longer felt scared, but exhilarated somehow. It was like flying.

"Hey, let me have another go," Ruby said as I started to slow.

Ruby handed me the beer and I gave her back the rope. For the rest of the afternoon we took turns in swinging from the broken-down staircase and sharing the beer.

When it was near dark, Winnie refastened the rope about the bannister and came back down the stairs.

"We should get going before someone notices we're missing," Ruby said. "If we're not back in our room by lights out, someone will come looking and then we'll be in all kinds of shit."

I brushed dust from the seat of my jeans and got up, heading back to the space in the wall where there had once been a front door.

"This way," Ruby said. "It's quicker."

I looked back to see her heading to the rear of the house. She climbed up onto the ledge of a broken window frame and climbed out of the house. I followed, finding myself in a field of bright yellow rapeseed.

"See?" Ruby said, pointing at the hill in the distance. "There's the orphanage. It's only five minutes across the field. I know a place where we can climb over the wall without being seen from the main building."

As we walked side by side back up the hill, I said, "Have you escaped loads of times before?"

"Got out of the orphanage you mean?"

"Yeah."

"Loads of times," she said with a wide grin.

"Ever been caught?"

"Loads of times," she beamed again.

"Don't you get into trouble?"

"Sometimes," she said, and I couldn't help but notice how quickly her smile had faded.

I wanted to ask what kind of trouble, but before I'd said anything, Ruby had taken my hand in hers. "Thanks," she said.

"For what?" I asked.

"For flying with me today," Ruby said, turning to look at the orphanage that stood on the brow of the hill in the growing darkness.

Chapter Fifteen

The orphanage was managed by two regular members of staff. Mr. Duvall and Miss Baxter. They both lived at the orphanage, just like the thirty girls in their care. Some of the girls said Mr. Duvall and Miss Baxter were shagging. Whether they were or not, I didn't know. What I did know for sure was they were both cruel at times and very odd. I had only been there a couple of weeks before I saw for myself how peculiar they could be.

Miss Baxter had been sitting at the front of the class filing down her fingernails and chewing on a piece of gum. She was about forty, I guessed, with hair pulled back into a bun and a pinched-looking face. She was a scrawny lady, with a hooked nose that looked more like a beak. Her eyes were black and beady, and she had lines about her mouth that made her lips looked puckered. As I'd spent most of my childhood being passed from one school, foster home, and care home to another, I'd never really stayed in one place long enough to learn much. This had affected my ability to read and write. I struggled with it. I'd come across a particular part in a book that I was reading. I raised my hand to ask for help. Several minutes passed and my arm began to ache.

Eventually, I called out and said, "Miss."

The woman seated at the front of the class didn't look up. Her fingernails seemed way more important than actually helping the girls in her class.

"Miss," I called out again, this time I clicked my fingers together to draw her attention.

At last she looked up and saw me. She put down her nail file and finally made her away across the class toward me. I lowered my aching arm and rubbed my muscles in an attempt to dispel the pins and needles that had started to tingle in them.

I looked up at her as she stood in front of me. I was just about to put the question to her that I had so long waited to ask, when to my complete surprise and shock, she slapped me across my face. I heard a cracking sound as my head rolled backwards under the force of her blow. My left cheek immediately began to burn with pain and glow hot. I looked at her completely stunned.

"Don't you ever click your fingers at me again, you insolent girl!" she barked.

I raised my hand to my face and it felt hot to the touch. The burning sensation crept its way around my jawline and down my neck. Without another word, she turned on her heels, went back to her desk, picked up the nail file, and started to preen herself again.

Most of the other girls in the class had turned to look at me, and my other cheek began to glow red as I flushed with embarrassment. I felt tears beginning to sting at the corners of my eyes and I wiped them away. I turned to look at Ruby, who was seated next to me.

"Don't worry about the old cow," she whispered. "She probably didn't get laid last night!" A huge smile crawled across her angelic face. Then, reaching out, she gently squeezed my hand with hers.

I also started to dread sports, as did most of the other girls, as Miss Baxter seemed to have some rather peculiar rules. One of these was that you always had to have a shower after sports, there were no excuses. Even if you hadn't a clean towel, you were expected to dry yourself with the clothes you would have to spend the rest of the day wearing.

After every lesson, Miss Baxter would insist that we all

stand naked in the changing room. Once we were all undressed, she would then lead us into the shower block, instructing us to leave our towels in the changing room. Once we had gathered in the shower block she would disappear momentarily to turn on the water. She would then reappear and stand by the door and watch us as we showered. I remember always feeling incredibly uncomfortable as she watched from the door, and I guessed most of the other girls did as well. It was like we were on show somehow. It fucking creeped me out.

Miss Baxter would disappear to turn off the water and reappear at the door again. Once or twice I caught her glancing up into the far corner of the ceiling of the shower, then back at us again. I followed her stare once, but all I could see was a row of cracked tiles. Once we had showered, she would make us form a queue, and one by one she would beckon us forward. Miss Baxter would then place one of her hands on the top of our heads and look us up and down. Once she was satisfied that you were clean enough, she would tell you to go back to the changing room. If you were unfortunate enough not to meet her high standards of cleanliness, you were made to go through the whole procedure again.

Once we had returned, we were not allowed to pick up our towel and start drying ourselves until she had reappeared in the room. Watching us from the door, Miss Baxter would then say, "Okay, girls, you may now start to dry yourselves."

If any girls objected and complained about her creepy behaviour, they would be sent to Mr. Duvall. He ran the orphanage. None of the girls who got sent to his office complained again. They seemed to forevermore wear a haunted look – like their spirit and strength had been sapped from them.

But Mr. Duvall was odd, too. He would take us for French and I dreaded every lesson with him. His behaviour toward the girls at the orphanage and how he sometimes conducted himself in front of us was only what I can describe as disturbing. I guessed he was in his mid-forties, with jet-black hair, which was always greased down on top of his head to hide the bald patch that was there. He wore far too much aftershave, which if he came too close would make me want to gag. Most of the lessons were spent with him sitting at the front of the class smarming down his hair and spraying himself with aftershave that he kept in his desk drawer. The thought of actually teaching us any French seemed to be way down on his list of priorities. Instead he would like to play this weird game with us. None of us could speak French. Most of us struggled to read and write English, let alone a foreign language. But all the same, Mr Duvall would challenge us to translate words and phrases that he had chosen into French. During my first couple of weeks at the orphanage, I heard rumours that if a girl failed to translate English into French correctly, he would make you put on lipstick as punishment. I'd found it hard to believe this rumour until one day I witnessed it for myself.

We had been learning to write and speak French in the past tense. Mr. Duvall picked on a girl named Carla Jones and said, "Tell me about a favourite place you went to when your parents were still alive."

Carla, who was about fourteen, sat thoughtfully for a moment and nervously played with the split ends of her red hair. "I went to a theme park," she eventually said.

"Okay, now say that again, but this time in French," Mr. Duvall said, taking the bottle of aftershave from his desk drawer and spraying around his head like he was warning off a swarm of invisible wasps.

Carla didn't reply immediately and I could see by the concentration on her face that she was trying to work out the translation.

"Come on, Jones, we don't have all day," Mr Duvall said with a tinge of impatience in his voice.

"J'ai alle...parc...d'attractions," Carla mumbled.

"I would like a full and accurate translation please, Jones. Not whatever it was you just said."

Carla began to fidget in her seat and she tried again. "J'ai alle...parc...d'attractions?"

"Non, non, non!" Mr. Duvall shouted. *"Je suis allais au parc d'attractions! Je suis allais au parc d'attractions!* That's the correct translation."

I could see Carla had turned scarlet with embarrassment and her freckles stood out like large muddy blotches all over her pale face.

"I think you need to be taught a lesson. Step out here," Mr. Duvall ordered her.

Carla slowly rose from her seat and made her way to the front of the class. She stood upright, hands by her sides. Mr. Duvall rummaged through the top drawer of his desk and produced a tub of foundation make-up. He dabbed a little pad into the tub then smeared the foundation across Carla's cheeks.

"There you go! You look a lot better already. Let's cover up those hideous freckles," he teased.

I couldn't believe what I was witnessing, and I looked at Ruby. She sat beside me, face pale and looking straight ahead.

Although it wasn't me being degraded in such a way, I couldn't help but feel sad and angry all at the same time for Carla.

"You look so pretty now," Mr. Duvall sighed, as he stood looking at Carla.

I didn't know whether he was being cruel of if he really did think Carla looked pretty now. Mr. Duvall turned and went back to his drawer.

"Let me see, what else do I have in here? Ah, yes! A nice *rouge* lipstick, it will go so well with that lovely ginger hair of yours!"

As I sat and watched him unscrew the lipstick, I couldn't help but wonder if it was the same make of lipstick that Ruby had given me to use. Had she stolen it from Mr. Duvall's desk? He unscrewed the lipstick then leaning in close – too close – to Carla, Mr. Duvall daubed her lips with it. Carla turned her head away. Mr. Duvall grabbed hold of Carla's face with his free hand, squeezing her cheeks together and puckering up her lips to make his task easier. He continued to apply the lipstick in big circular motions as Carla fruitlessly tried to pull her face away. The more she struggled, the more make-up Mr. Duvall applied.

I glanced around the room and at the other girls seated at their desks. They sat like statues, as if too scared to move for fear of drawing Mr. Duvall's attention to them.

With his hand still gripping Carla's face so tight that her now bright red and gaudy lips protruded outwards, Mr. Duvall stared at her. His eyes almost seemed to glaze over – like he was imagining himself to be someplace else. As if imagining something else altogether.

"Those lips look good enough to kiss," he whispered, that odd look still on his face.

Carla flinched backwards as if fearing what was going to happen next.

"Give me a little kiss," he said.

Carla shook her head, even though he still gripped her face.

"Go on," he smiled, turning his cheek toward her. "Just one little kiss. It won't hurt."

Carla turned her head away and I caught a look of revulsion on her face. I wanted to stand up and scream at Mr.

Duvall. I wanted to tell him to stop. I pushed back my chair, but before I'd had a chance to stand, I felt Ruby's hand fall over mine. She didn't look at me. She didn't have to. For someone so small, her grip was surprisingly strong as she stopped me from getting up out of my chair.

Knowing that Carla would never kiss him of her own free will, Mr. Duvall leant slowly forward, his shadow falling over her, and kissed her on the mouth. His lips lingered against hers as she twisted her head left then right. Slowly he leaned back and I could see that his eyes were closed. His hand fell away from Carla's face. She immediately turned and hurried back to her desk, smearing the lipstick – or his kiss – away with her fingers. I couldn't help but notice how the thick foundation he had covered her freckles with was now glistening with her tears.

"Go back to your rooms," Mr. Duvall whispered.

Silently we stood and filed out of the room. As I went, I saw how Mr. Duvall watched Carla go – not taking his eyes off her once.

I shared a room with Ruby at the orphanage, and that's where we headed after Mr. Duvall had dismissed us from his lesson. Ruby sat on her bed, red coat on, knees drawn up beneath her chin. I sat on my bed and looked out the window. I was upset by what I had seen. Was Mr. Duvall just a letch, or was he more than that? I knew stuff like that went on. Every other day I'd heard stories told by kids of the abuse they had suffered at the hands of carers in children's homes. But I had never seen anything like that. I couldn't rid my mind of how scared and revolted Carla had looked as Mr. Duvall had covered her mouth with lipstick, and I wished that there had been some way I could've stopped it. I looked out the window and across the small courtyard where both Mr. Duvall and Miss Baxter had their rooms – where they lived. I felt gooseflesh crawl over me and I looked away and back at Ruby.

Even though she was small for her age, she had always seemed full of so much energy and life. But not now. She looked like a tiny doll lost in a coat that was way too big for her.

"Hey, Ruby," I said, getting up from my bed and crossing the room. I sat down next to her.

She didn't look up.

"That lipstick you had the other day, did you take it from Duvall's desk drawer?" I asked. "And what about the money?"

Ruby said nothing.

"It's okay, I won't tell…" I started.

Then pulling her hood up over her head, she rolled onto her side, her back to the room. "I don't want to talk about it," she said.

I took a deep breath, my heart racing. "Did Duvall…"

"Leave me alone," she whispered. "Just leave me alone."

Slowly, I got up from her bed and went back to my own. Lying down, I rolled onto my side and closed my eyes tight. I didn't want to imagine how Ruby had come by that lipstick. I couldn't bear to think that she had been given that money by someone to buy her silence. With fresh tears growing in my eyes, and knowing that I need to start running again, I let the tiredness I now felt take me.

I don't know for how long I'd been asleep. But when I opened my eyes again, the room was in darkness. The glow from the courtyard lights glared through my windows. Perhaps it had been the light that had disturbed me. I sat up and looked across the room. Ruby was asleep, still curled on her side, hood pulled up over her head. As quietly as I could, I got out of bed and went to the window to draw the curtains to block out the glare of the light from the courtyard. It was then I heard the sound of sobbing. At first I thought perhaps it was coming from behind me – from where Ruby lay huddled on the bed in the far corner of our room. But the sound of crying was coming from outside. Peering around the edge of the curtain, I watched as Miss Baxter led Carla Jones from the building where Mr. Duvall had his accommodation.

"Everything is going to be okay," I heard Miss Baxter tell Carla, leading her across the courtyard and toward the building where I secretly watched them from.

Carefully, so as not to be seen, I pulled the curtains and dropped down onto my bed. Sleep didn't come easy again that night.

Chapter Sixteen

Ruby and I spent the next day together. She seemed brighter somehow. I wanted to tell her what I had seen from my window and ask her again about how she came by the lipstick and money. But I was scared that if I asked too much and too soon, I might only cause her to clam up again like she had before. After all, she might have come across the money and lipstick quiet innocently, but I doubted that.

I might not have been able to read and write very well, but I had been around the track enough times to have a good idea of what Mr. Duvall was up to at the orphanage. But after last night, I wasn't sure if Miss Baxter, despite her strange behaviour, was trying to help the girls or, like Duvall, harm them in some way. Whatever the case, my first thought was to run again, but I couldn't. As I had lay awake that night unable to sleep, I knew that if I were to run, I would take Ruby with me. I wouldn't leave her behind. But where would we go? How would we look after ourselves? There were as many dangers on the other side of the orphanage walls as there were on the inside. The choices I had made before in my short life hadn't always been the right ones – but they had been my choices and had only affected me. And besides, I knew that if I took Ruby with me, she would become my responsibility. It wasn't that I was scared of. What scared me was letting her down. Leading her into more danger somehow. I thought about going to the authorities – to the police – but I'd known other kids like me who had done that before. They were rarely believed. We came from troubled backgrounds. Made up lies about the adults we resented for laying down some rules and discipline in our chaotic lives. I knew of many a kid who had been returned to the very people who had been hurting them, only to find out the abuse was now much worse.

I knew that I would have to figure out some kind of plan – some way of leaving the orphanage and taking my friend Ruby with me. So pretending, just like Ruby, that there was nothing wrong at the orphanage, we set off across the field, over the wall, and made toward the house with the makeshift swing. It was cold and we wrapped our coats tight about us. The sky was a threatening grey and I wondered if we might not have some snow. Snow was okay as long as you had someplace nice and warm to shelter from it. It was not much fun otherwise. I looked up at the purple coloured sky, then back at the orphanage on top of the hill behind us. However much I now feared what was taking place there, I also feared our chances if we decided to run in the middle of winter.

With my hands tucked into my coat sleeves, I followed Ruby across the field toward the derelict farmhouse at the bottom of the hill. Following her through the broken window frame, the stench inside seemed stronger than I'd remembered it to be. Ruby suddenly stopped ahead of me.

"Look!" she gasped, throwing one hand to her face and pointing into the corner of the room with the other.

Looking past her, I gasped too, taking a step backwards. A gust of wind blew in through the empty door and window frames, blowing the fringe from the face of a teenaged boy who lay slumped in the corner. His moving hair gave the appearance that he was alive, but I could tell by the waxy sheen of his skin that he was dead. He was emaciated. His face was like a skull that had been wrapped with paper-thin flesh, mottled blue and mauve. He lay slumped against the wall, his eyes black and open. It was like he was watching us from the corner of the room. His denim-clad legs spread wide, and one sleeve of his dirty shirt was rolled to the elbow. A thin leather belt had been tightened about his forearm, and the crook of his elbow was scarred black and blue with old puncture marks. A thick, white, crusty scab of mucus covered his nostrils and upper lip.

I looked away. I was scared. Not of him, but of how he'd died – how so many of the young people I had met had died. Those of us who decided to run. I glanced through the broken window and back up the hill where the orphanage loomed. Had this young boy run from such a place? Is this how either Ruby or myself might end up if we ran, too? Would either of us be found dead one day in such a godforsaken place, dead from drugs – anything to block out what we had run from, and even worse what we had run to? I looked back at the dead teenaged boy and he was a reminder of the stark reality of the kind of life I could be leading Ruby into if I escaped from the orphanage with her. I wasn't sure I wanted that responsibly nor the responsibility of fleeing without her and leaving her in the care of Mr. Duvall.

"His name was Brian," Ruby suddenly said.

"You knew him?" I whispered.

"He made the swing," she said, turning away.

I watched her head to the empty doorway. "Where you going?"

"To get the police," she said, stopping to look back at me. A gust of wind blew hard from outside, dead winter leaves flitting about her worn shoes.

"The police will just take us back to the orphanage and Duvall will know..." I started, not wanting to be caught on the other side of the orphanage walls by him and fearing what our punishment might be.

"I can't just leave him," Ruby said. "He was my friend. Friends don't run out on each other – not even when they're dead."

Turning, and with her hood up, she left the old farmhouse.

We were both gasping for breath by the time we crashed through the door of the town's small police station. I had run all the way behind Ruby as she had raced away from the farmhouse and into town. Ruby frantically hit the front counter bell over and over again with her fist in a desperate attempt to attract someone's attention. A police officer appeared from the back office and approached the counter. His uniform was crisp and clean with gleaming stripes on each shoulder. Ruby continued to ring the bell as if she hadn't noticed him.

"Easy, girl, you're gonna break it," he said, placing his hand over Ruby's. The ringing became muffled at once then stopped altogether. "Where's the fire?"

"We've found a body!" Ruby gasped.

"Where?" he asked, eyeing her carefully up and down.

"In that old farmhouse out on Orchard Road," Ruby explained.

"You'd better show me," he said, snatching up his hat and marching around from the other side of the counter.

We climbed into the back of his police car as he sped us away in the direction of where we had found the body. The last time I'd been in a police car was after I'd been picked up by the cops after running from yet another care home.

The police officer slowed as he reached the gap in the road that led to the farmhouse. The track was too narrow for him to steer the police car along it.

"This is as far as we go," he said, pushing open his door and climbing out. Wedging his hat back on the crown of his head, he let us out. We led him along the track and back toward the house. Ruby walked ahead, the red hood of her coat pulled up against the wind that was now icy cold.

"He's inside. In the corner," Ruby said, stopping at the gap where a door would have once been.

"Okay, girls, you just wait right here," the officer said.

We watched him make his way inside, the sound of his boots clattering with old beer cans and bottles. He hadn't been gone very long, when he appeared in the doorway again. Without looking at us, the officer took his radio from his belt and spoke into it, notifying his colleagues and control room what he had found.

Within half an hour of us arriving back at the farmhouse, the immediate area had been roped off with blue and white striped police tape. A couple of uniformed officers kept guard at the edge of this cordon. One of them had a clipboard and pen and recorded the details of everyone who entered and left the scene. Ruby stood to one side and watched the police officers come and go from the house. A black van arrived. Two men in black suits got out and took a stretcher from the back of it. They went inside what was left of the old farmhouse. A short time later, they reappeared. I could see the black body bag on the stretcher. I knew that Ruby's friend Brian was inside it. Without looking at her, I reached out and took her hand in mine, just like she had taken mine before.

"C'mon," I said softly, leading her away from the house and back into the field behind it. "Let's get going before that cop starts asking too many questions."

That night as I lay in bed, struggling to get to sleep, I felt Ruby slide into bed beside me. Without saying anything, I slid my arms about her, holding her tight. I couldn't ever imagine either of us wanting to go back to that house again. But we did. We had no choice about that.

Chapter Seventeen

It had snowed during the night. Giant drifts of white had formed against the grey stone walls of the orphanage. When I looked out of my window all I could see were the white fields and hills rolling away into the distance. The world seemed so quiet. It was like the white blanket of snow that now covered everything had muffled out the sound. After breakfast we made our way down to the changing rooms and showers. Our sports lesson with Miss Baxter hadn't been cancelled despite the freezing cold weather and snowfall.

The thirty or so girls who lived at the orphanage huddled together in the changing room. Miss Baxter stood leaning against the tiled wall watching us. As I hurriedly changed into a pair of grubby shorts and T-shirt, I noticed that Carla Jones was frantically searching through the small bag that she kept her sportswear in.

"Are you okay?" I asked her.

"I can't find my shorts," she whispered, still searching the bottom of her bag.

"What's all the fuss over there?" I heard Miss Baxter ask.

I glanced back over my shoulder to see her step away from the wall.

"I've left my shorts in my room," Carla said, her face white with dread. "Please may I go back to fetch them, Miss Baxter?"

"No need," Miss Baxter said with a smile. "I have a special pair of shorts for girls like you."

She sauntered across the changing room, stopping in front of Carla, who now cowered before her. "You can wear these."

Carla looked down at Miss Baxter's empty hands and frowned. "I don't understand," Carla breathed.

"They're magic shorts," Baxter smiled again. "They're *invisible*."

"But..." Carla started.

"But nothing, girl," Miss Baxter said, her face looking more wizened and cruel than I'd ever seen it. "You know the rules. If you don't bring shorts with you, then you'll have to do the lesson in your underwear."

"But it's freezing," Carla said. I guessed the cold wasn't the only reason Carla didn't want to parade about in the snow in just her underwear. "Can't I just go back to my room and get my...?"

"No," Miss Baxter said with a slow shake of her head, eyes gleaming. "Now get undressed for lesson."

Without saying anything more, Carla snatched up her bag, clutching it to her chest, and headed toward the door.

"What do you think you are doing, girl?" Baxter snapped, making a whistling noise through her nose.

"I'm not wearing just my underwear. I'm going back to my room to get my shorts," Carla said.

"Come back here,' Baxter insisted. "You'll do as I say. You won't ever forget your shorts again, I can promise you that."

"I'm going to get my shorts!" Carla suddenly screamed, spinning around and facing Miss Baxter.

We all stopped changing and stood looking at Carla and Miss Baxter.

"Don't argue with me, girl. You'll wear your underwear for sports today!" Baxter whined.

Carla glanced around the changing room, suddenly aware that we were all looking at her. She was centre of attention and for all the wrong reasons again. I could see tears begin to well in her eyes and I couldn't help but feel desperately sorry for her.

Then without warning, Carla made a fist with her hand and punched Miss Baxter squarely in the face. An immediate and collective gasp escaped from the mouths of all us as we watched Miss Baxter stagger backwards, hands to her face. Shaking her head as if dazed, she lowered her hands and looked at the blood that gushed from her nose now splattering the floor of the changing room.

"You little bitch. After I tried to comfort you last night," she grimaced. She grabbed for Carla's hair with her blood-stained hands. Carla rocked back on her heels and out of Baxter's reach.

"Why don't you leave Carla alone," I heard someone say.

It was then I noticed Ruby had disappeared from my side and was standing in front of Carla and looking up at Miss Baxter.

"Get out of my way," Baxter said, towering over Ruby. She shoved Ruby aside, knocking her to the floor.

"Hey!" I shouted. "Don't you dare touch my friend! What gives you the fucking right?" I said, stepping away from the clothes hooks and approaching Baxter. Even though I was just fifteen, I was as tall as her.

Baxter looked back at me, and for the briefest of moments I thought I saw a glimmer of uncertainty in her eyes – it could have even been fear. What if we all turned on her? What if all the girls she and Mr. Duvall had treated so badly suddenly turned on her? Those were the questions I wondered if she was asking herself in that split second before the door to the changing room flew open with such force I feared there had been some kind of an explosion.

With a murderous look on his face and his eyes black with anger, Mr. Duvall scowled at the class. "Right, you lot! Get in the gym. I want fifty press-ups, fifty squat-thrusts, fifty pull-ups, and God forbid I come back and find any of you slacking! Now get going."

Without saying a word, the girls sauntered out, some of them sneaking sideways glances at us as they left, as if they expected never to see Ruby, Carla, or me again. Once we were alone with Miss Baxter and Mr Duvall, he roared, "I will not put up with such behaviour."

How had he known what had happened? I wondered. The door had been shut and there were no windows that he could have seen through.

He looked at Baxter, her top lip black with blood. "Miss Baxter, take Carla to my office. I will deal with her later."

I stood next to Ruby as Miss Baxter seized Carla by the arm and dragged her from the changing room. I wanted Miss Baxter to stop. And I would have told her to do so if Mr. Duvall hadn't been looming nearby, his aftershave smelling like sweat and onions. Miss Baxter I believed I could have fought with and won, but Duvall was a different proposition altogether. I suspected that he could hurt me and Ruby in other ways than just hitting us. To be honest, I was scared of him and what he was capable of. Just his presence seemed to sap any rebellion from me.

"Right, you two, follow me," he roared.

Ruby snatched up her coat and we followed him out of the changing room and onto the field. As soon as the door leading outside was opened, I was immediately struck by a blast of freezing cold air. Gooseflesh immediately crawled its way up my arms and legs like a ravenous disease. Duvall led us onto the sports field as I wrapped my arms about myself and the snow crunched crisply beneath my worn-out trainers. I glanced at Ruby and she too had folded her arms around herself, huddled beneath her red coat. I wore nothing more than a T-shirt and flimsy shorts. It was absolutely bitter. The sky hung darkly above us, looking battered and bruised, getting ready to belch another huge throat full of snow over us.

We followed Mr. Duvall into the centre of the field, becoming disorientated and lost in our white barren surroundings. Streams of breath plumed from our mouths and nostrils and my feet began to ache with the cold. He stopped and so did we.

We stood shivering before him. "You surprise me, Ruby Little. I thought we had an understanding."

"We've never had an understanding," she said back, teeth chattering now with the cold.

His eyes narrowed. "You like seeing people being punched, do you? Think it's fun for someone to punch Miss Baxter in the face, do you?" he asked Ruby.

She looked down at the snow that covered her trainers.

"Punch your friend Winnie in the mouth for me, or I'll tell her all about the special understanding me and you have," he said.

"You wouldn't," Ruby said unbelievingly.

"Try me," Duvall threatened.

Before I knew what had happened, Ruby had punched me in the mouth. My lip rolled back and smashed into my teeth, causing it to instantly swell and bleed. I blinked in disbelief at Ruby as I dabbed at my bleeding mouth with my frozen fingers. I searched her eyes and she looked at me.

"I said *punch* her, not tickle her!" Duvall shouted over the cry of the wind.

"I'm sorry, Winnie," Ruby said, striking me in the face again, but this time harder than before. I lost my footing and staggered backwards into the bitter snow. I felt a warm sensation on my top lip and chin. I put a hand to my face and wiped away the blood that was now gushing from my nose in a thick stream.

"I'm not going to fight you, Ruby," I said. "That's what he wants. Whatever he is going to tell me about you, I don't care. I know none of it was your fault. You have nothing to feel ashamed of," I told her.

"Hit her again, Ruby, don't just stand there!" Duvall shouted.

"I can't. Winnie's my friend," Ruby told him.

"What about the lipstick and the money..." Duvall hadn't even finished, before Ruby was on top of me punching my face, arms, legs, and body. I screwed myself up into a ball as the snow worked its icy hands down my shorts and up my T-shirt.

"I won't fight back, Ruby!" I cried from beneath her reign of blows.

"...What about the lipstick... should I tell her about the money and what you did for it...?" continued in the background.

As Ruby's fists connected with my aching body, I heard her start to cry. Through her sobs, I could hear Ruby whispering over and over again:

"I'm sorry! I'm sorry! I love you, Winnie, I do love you!"

Even though I understood why she was attacking me, and I could hear her crying, I began to feel hate toward her. I tried desperately to overcome those feelings but they were consuming me. I was freezing cold, I could see splashes of my own blood staring gruesomely at me from the pure white snow, and my whole body pulsated in pain. I hated Ruby for all of it. But that was what Duvall wanted. He wanted me to hate Ruby. He didn't want us to be friends. He feared that. He feared not what I might learn about Ruby, but what Ruby might tell me about him.

So as I lay there, buried under her reign of blows and the wet blanket of snow, I knew that Duvall was scared. He was scared of anyone who might stand up to him. He was scared of anyone who might stand up to what he was doing to the girls at the orphanage. He was like every other bully I'd ever met. He was nothing more than a coward. And to know that made me smile. Because I knew I had him beat. And gradually that smile turned into a grin – a snigger – a laugh. Clutching my belly, not through pain but deep, uncontrollable belly laughs, I roared and roared. Hot steaming tears warmed my face. I managed to steal a glance at Ruby, her punches starting to soften and slow. Behind her, I could see Duvall looking at the both of us. He had a perplexed expression clawing at his pointed face.

I then began to hear Ruby laugh. It was slight at first, just a few giggles. Then, like me, she began to laugh uncontrollably. Ruby flopped off me and rolled over in the snow. We looked at Duvall and he looked beaten. Ruby and I glanced at each other and we knew we had won. I threw my arm around Ruby and hollered at the top of my voice so it echoed like thunder around the sports field, *"I love you, Ruby Little! I love you, and nothing will ever change that!"*

With arms about each other, we got to our feet and stood shivering before Mr. Duvall. We continued to laugh, our arms slung defiantly around each other's shoulders. We looked at Duvall who stood, snow now falling all about him.

"You freaks," he whispered, lunging forward, his face an angry snarl. He yanked us apart.

Ruby fell one way and I another. I looked back to see Duvall standing over me, snow now covering his smarmed-down hair and shoulders. "You will learn to respect me," he hissed, reaching down for me. I clawed at his arms and hands as he tried to pull me to my feet.

"Get offa me!" I screamed, kicking out with my legs. Glancing to my right, I could see Ruby lying face first in the snow. Was she injured? Had she hurt herself falling down? Was she unconscious? "Ruby!"

Duvall's grip was vice-like as he crushed his fingers about my arm. He dragged me back toward the school. "You need to be broken," he seethed.

"Fuck off!" I screamed, bringing up my knee and driving it

into his groin.

His eyes bulged in their sockets like two hardboiled eggs, just white as they rolled back in their sockets. His mouth hung open as he let go of me and gripped his balls. "Bitch," he gasped.

Turning, I fled. I raced back toward the place I had last seen Ruby. But the snow was falling so hard and fast now, that I couldn't be sure I was heading in the right direction. The sky was so overcast that it appeared almost to be night. Snow pelted my face, arms and legs. I felt so cold I could hardly draw breath.

"Ruby!" I screamed. Wet strands of my hair blew across my face and I clawed them away as I fought to find my friend. I looked back over my shoulder trying to get my bearings. Which way was I to go? What was I to do? Then like some demonic phantom, Duval loomed toward me out of the blizzard. I screamed, staggering backwards. Drawing in lungfuls of freezing cold air, I turned and fled, leaving Ruby somewhere behind me in the snow.

Chapter Eighteen

I ran and ran, Duval panting behind me. My legs ached with cold and tiredness as I trudged through the deepening snow. Glancing back, I could see him just feet away, his hair white now, the only colour was his crimson leer.

"I will break you," he shouted. "You will be broken."

I pushed forward as hard and as fast as I could, using every ounce of the little energy I had left. I felt numb with cold and fear. I knew that if Duvall caught me, he would hurt me bad. My life would never be the same. I would never be the same. I'd have that hollow look I'd seen on Carla's face as Miss Baxter had led her from Duvall's apartment.

Through the snow, I thought I saw something that I recognised and staggered toward it. Reaching out, I pressed my hands flat against the rough stone wall that surrounded the orphanage. I was sure this was the place where Ruby and I had climbed over when we snuck out. With Duvall just inches away now, I scrambled up the wall. My fingers were so cold now, that I could barely feel the rough, uneven brick beneath them. I found a jagged piece of stone jutting from the wall and used it to leaver myself up. I searched blindly with my fingertips for the top of the wall. An icy hand wrapped itself around my ankle as I was yanked downwards. Looking down, I could see that Duvall had hold of me. I kicked out wildly with my free foot, driving it down into his face. Crying out, he fell onto his arse into the snow. Seeing my chance, I reached up, my fingers finding the top of the wall. Screaming out, I pulled myself up, my fear forcing me on. I scrambled over to see Duval back on his feet and climbing the wall after me.

Too tired to climb down the other side of the wall, I just let myself drop. I landed on my side, air exploding from deep within my lungs. Winded and in pain, I crawled away from the wall and down the hill. My hair hung wet against the sides of my frozen face. I glanced at my hands and they looked like two raw slabs of meat. My legs had turned a bluey-mauve with the cold. The sound of Duvall dropping from the wall and into the snow behind me forced me on. Clawing myself to my feet, I staggered forward the snow, the wind driving mercilessly into my face and body. Raising one numb hand I placed it over my eyes and peered ahead. All I could see was a world of whiteness.

I looked back to see Duval coming down the hill toward me. Turning, I staggered on. With the last of my strength and will to carry on being sapped by the cold, wind, and snow, I thought I saw something ahead. It was dark and square. The rundown farmhouse I had visited with Ruby. I lurched toward it, teeth chattering uncontrollably up and down with cold and terror. Reaching the glassless broken window frame, I climbed up and inside. The wind howled through its derelict walls and open doorways, but there was no snow. That was something. I glanced into the corner where Ruby and I had discovered her friend Brian. It was like he had never been there. The area was still littered with empty beer cans, needles, and cigarette ends.

Gasping out loud, I turned to see Duval scrambling through the open window into the farmhouse. Spinning around and looking for someplace to hide, I saw the unstable staircase. Moving carefully, but as quickly as I could, I climbed up into the darkness. The stairs creaked with every step I took, giving my location away. I reached the top, cowering on the landing. From below I could hear the sound of Duvall's shoes on the old wooden floorboards as he searched the farmhouse for me.

"Winnie," he teased. *"Winneeeee!"*

Peering around the edge of the bannister, I saw his

shadow fall over the bottom stair. I crawled backwards and stifled a scream as something brushed up against my face. I peered into the darkness and could see that it was just the end of the blue rope that Ruby and I had swung on. The bottom stair creaked and I knew that I had given my hiding place away as Duvall slowly climbed the stairs.

With nowhere else to go, I cowered in the darkness as he loomed at the top of the stairs. Seeing me there, Duvall smiled. And although he looked as cold and dishevelled as I did, he wore a smile. A smile of triumph knowing that he had me.

"I will break you," he said, his fingers going to his belt where he began to fumble it open. "You will learn to respect me, just like the others – just like Ruby."

Drawing my knees up to my chest and wrapping my arms tight about me like a closed flower, I screamed. *"Don't you touch me! Don't you fucking dare!"*

Letting his trousers drop to his ankles, Duvall stood over me. "Just like Ruby, you'll get used to the money, the make-up. All girls like to make themselves look pretty, don't they?"

"You made me feel ugly!" I heard someone scream.

I looked through Duvall's legs to see Ruby come running down the landing like a bright red flash of light in her coat. With palms out she clattered into Duvall, sending him sprawling onto the floor. I crawled to one side, not wanting to be near him – not wanting to be touched by him – even by chance.

Duvall pulled himself up on to his knees, desperate to get back to his feet, but stumbled forward again, trousers knotted about his ankles. Ruby reached for the blue rope, unfastened it from the banister, slipping the end that had been fashioned into something like a noose and placed it over Duvall's head, then neck. Duvall threw his hands to his throat, as Ruby pulled tight on the rope. He clawed at it with his fingers.

"I never wanted your money and all those other gifts!" she screamed at him. "It wasn't the money and the make-up that bought my silence, it was fear. It was my fear of you. But I'm not scared of you anymore. I won't be silent again. I won't be silent so you can hurt my friend Winnie."

On his knees, face turning blue and clawing at the noose about his throat, he tried to get to his feet. Ruby let go of the rope as he lurched forward, trousers ensnaring his ankles. In the gloom he stumbled toward the banister – toward the edge of the stairs. He made a gargling sound as he tried to loosen the rope about his neck.

"You'll never hurt me again!" Ruby screamed, running forward, hands out, shoving Duvall in the back. "You'll never hurt another girl again."

With his arms flapping like a set of wings on either side of him, Duvall spilled over the edge of the stairs and dropped out of sight. I screwed my eyes shut and covered my ears at the crunch of his neck breaking.

As if her legs had been kicked from beneath her, Ruby slid down the landing wall. With her arms locked tight about her, she sat and rocked back and forth, the unmistakeable sound of sobs coming from beneath her hood. Shaking from head to foot, I slowly crawled along the landing toward her. Cradling Ruby Little in my arms, I whispered, "Thank you for saving me, Ruby. Thank you for saving all of us." I held her tight and didn't let go until it had turned full dark outside.

Part Three

Winnie

Chapter Nineteen

Just like Winnie had held Ruby Little, Thaddeus now cradled Winnie in his arms. The train continued to rock from side to side as it passed over track points, making its way north toward Scotland.

"What happened to you both?" Thaddeus asked. "Did anyone ever find out what happened in the old farmhouse that night?"

"As I sat in the dark with Ruby," Winnie started to explain, "she told me everything that had taken place at the orphanage. Both Baxter and Duvall had been abusing the girls in their care. Ruby couldn't be sure, but she thought that Baxter and Duvall had been lovers too. Baxter kinda groomed the girls. That's what she was doing during sports lessons – why she was asking us to parade back and forth naked between the shower block and changing rooms. Duvall had been hiding in the floor space over the showers. As Ruby told me this, I understood why I had caught Miss Baxter looking up at the ceiling and why the tiles had been cracked there. Ruby said that Duvall sometimes filmed through the hole on his mobile phone. I asked her how she knew this, and Ruby told me that Duvall had shown footage of her on his phone. He then threatened that if she didn't do as he said, he would upload the film on the Internet. Knowing that Duvall had footage of them was bad enough, let alone he might share it with others, too. So they went along with whatever he demanded. He had favourites, of which Ruby was one, and he bought their silence by giving them pocket money and buying them gifts, like perfume and make-up."

"Did anyone ever find out that Ruby had killed Duvall?"

Thaddeus asked.

"No, it stayed our secret," Winnie whispered, as if still afraid that someone might discover the truth. "We knew we could never go back to the orphanage, but the other girls were still in the care of Miss Baxter, and sooner or later someone would raise the alarm that Duvall was missing. So as we crept from the farmhouse, Ruby stopped halfway up the stairs where Duvall hung. With her eyes closed, as if still too scared to touch him although he would never be able to hurt her again, Ruby reached out and took Duvall's mobile phone from the pocket of his trousers.

"Together we made our way through the dark, the snow, and back to the police station. It was locked when we got there, as the police officer we had dealt with before was out on patrol. Taking the phone, Ruby posted it through the letterbox. She knew what that police officer would eventually find on it and it would lead him to the orphanage, Miss Baxter, and the truth of what had been taking place there. Sooner or later someone would find Duvall, just like we had found Ruby's friend Brian in that farmhouse.

"Hand in hand we turned our back on that small town and the orphanage on top of the hill. A few days later we read in a newspaper that Duvall's body had been found. His death was being treated as a suicide. It was believed that he had taken his own life as he feared the abuse of young girls he had been involved in was about to come to light. His accomplice, Miss Baxter, was arrested and charged. The orphanage was closed down. Any girls who had been recorded as staying at the orphanage would be found and interviewed as potential witnesses and victims.

"Knowing that we never wanted to be found again, Ruby and I spent the next few days and weeks hitching our way to

London, believing that we would find jobs and a new and better life there. But it didn't turn out like that. We were homeless and lived on the streets. Ruby would disappear for days on end. When she returned, she didn't seem herself. Even the money she returned with didn't make her happy. It was like every time she came back, a little piece of her was missing. I knew she had started to take drugs given to her by the men she went with. It was like Duvall still had a hold over her. It was painful to watch and I seemed unable to help her. Bit by bit, we grew further apart. I met a guy who I lived with for a time, but he treated me bad too, so I went back to the streets. Ruby and I crossed paths again, and this time she seemed smaller and more fragile than I'd ever seen her before. We struck up our friendship again, but it was never the same. And although she had started to steal what little money I managed to beg, I just couldn't give up on her – or walk away. There was a part of me that believed I could've saved her – just like she had saved me that night from Duvall. I didn't want to… I didn't want…" Winnie made a hitching noise in the back of her throat as she fought back the tears filling her eyes.

"Didn't want to what?" Thaddeus asked gently.

"I didn't want to find her dead one day," Winnie sobbed into Thaddeus's chest. "I didn't want to find her overdosed on drugs like we had found Brian. I didn't want to see my beautiful little friend end up like that. Ruby deserved better. But I did find her just like that. Dead from drugs the night I came back from meeting you. I found her lying under those arches behind the Embankment Tube station."

As if too painful to remember, Winnie buried her face against Thaddeus as he held her tightly in her arms. "I'm so sorry," he whispered. "I'm so sorry, Winnie."

Chapter Twenty

With his muddy clothes drying over the side of the bath, Police Inspector Lance Stoke showered the dirt from his hair and off his body. However much his sergeant Becka Horton had slowed him down, he was glad that he hadn't killed her already, as she had saved him. Horton had not only saved Stoke, but the piece of Moonbeam he had snatched from Blake's ear. He had invited her back into his room so that perhaps he could thank her properly, and much to his surprise, Becka had smiled back at him and said that she might come to his room once he had washed off all the mud. With heart racing, he had watched her swish away down the corridor and disappear into her room. Why such a change of heart? Stoke had wondered, closing his own motel room door behind him. Horton had rejected every other advance he made toward her. Perhaps, like all the other women he had eventually taken, they had, in the end, been unable to resist him.

Standing naked and fresh from the shower, Stoke stood in the centre of his motel room. He picked up the chip of Moonbeam from off the bedside table where he had placed it next to his mobile phone. The piece of Moonbeam pulsed blue then white in his hand like a beacon. He looked at it, dark eyes growing wide in wonder at its power. Slowly, Stoke turned around in his room. He faced south, then west, then north. He stopped, heart starting to race. The piece of Moonbeam gleamed an almost neon blue in the palm of his hand. It felt as if it was beating somehow, as quick as his heart.

"North," he whispered to himself, realising that since hunting Blake, the wolf had always been heading north. "What's north?"

Placing the stone back down and snatching up his phone, Stoke sat on the edge of the bed. He pressed his brother's number into the keypad, then raised the phone to his ear. Stoke didn't even hear the phone ring once before it was answered by his brother, Josef, deep beneath the Carpathian Mountains.

His brother sounded out of breath. Panicked. "Tell me you have some good news, brother. I need something – anything to tell Nicodemus. He grows restless. Angry."

"I caught up with Blake. We fought…" Stoke started.

"You have him then?" Josef cut in.

"No, the wolf escaped," Stoke said.

"Then it is over – our lives are over…" Josef almost screeched.

"Listen to me," Stoke hissed into the phone. "Just listen to me. He might have got away from me, but not for long…"

"But…"

"You're not listening to me, Josef," Stoke said. "I have a piece of the Moonbeam. Tracking him will be easy. The wolf is heading north."

"North? Where North? *The north-fucking-pole?*" Josef almost screamed down the phone, his voice thick with panic and fear.

"I don't know exactly where," Stoke tried to soothe him. "But I'm closing in on him."

Stoke looked up at the sound of a sudden knock on his motel room door. "I'm going to have to go…"

"Go? Go?" Josef screeched again. "Go fucking where? I need something to tell Nico…"

"I'll call you tomorrow night," Stoke said, ending the call and placing the phone back down again.

From the hallway, Becka could hear Stoke talking. Leaning in close, she tried to hear what it was he was saying and who he was talking to. Was he updating the police control room? She doubted it. Her inspector usually left mundane jobs like that to her. She had already untied her hair from its bun and let it cascade darkly about her shoulders in thick waves. Before knocking on the door, she popped the top two buttons of her blouse open. She knew that killing Stoke was going to be all too easy. Just like every other man she had killed, he wouldn't be able to resist her. Smiling, she knocked on the door.

Stoke got up from the bed. His clothes were still drying in the bathroom and he had nothing on. The knock came again and he didn't need to look through the spyhole in the door to know who was on the other side. Horton had said she would come back. Come to him after he had washed away the mud, and he had done that. Dimming the lights, he went to the door, still unsure whether he would kill her or not. But one thing he knew for sure was that if she were ever to leave his room again, she would be like him. One of the living dead. Naked, Stoke opened the door. Looking him up and down, a smile crawled across her full mouth. Without saying anything, Becka stepped inside.

So easy, they both thought to themselves.

Pushing the door closed and trapping them both in near darkness, Stoke pushed Becka back toward the bed. He wasted no time clawing at her clothes.

"You have no idea how much I've waited for this moment," he breathed, pulling her close.

"I think I know," she smiled back.

Stoke paused, looking into her eyes. Had she really wanted him all along? Had Becka been hiding her true feelings from him? he wondered with excitement, his heart racing faster. He tore her shirt free and looked at her. She was more beautiful – her skin more soft and subtle looking than he had ever imagined.

He leant forward to kiss her mouth. She moved to meet his kiss. And with eyes still half open, readying to make her attack, she saw for the first time razor-sharp fangs sprout from Stoke's gums.

Vampire! she screamed inside.

Becka flinched, pulling back just a fraction, but enough for Stoke to sense something wasn't right. He opened his eyes and bulked backwards at the sight of Horton's face, which looked more wolf now than human.

"Lycan..." he stammered, a series of gargles in the back of his throat as Becka lunged forward, burying her snout into his neck.

With a vicious ferocity, Becka tore Stoke's throat out with one single bite. His head swung back, attached to his neck now by one single strip of flesh, so big was her bite. With blood drooling from her fur-covered snout and pumping from the gaping wound in his neck, Becka dragged Stoke's twitching body into the bathroom by her claws. Grunting and panting like a tired dog, she lifted Stoke's body, placing him into the bath. And while his body still felt warm and his heart thick with blood, she sunk one giant claw into his chest and cut out his heart.

Changing back into her human form, she strolled into the bedroom, eating the heart like it was nothing more than an overripe piece of fruit. She licked away a stream of blood from the corner of her mouth and sighed. Discovering that Stoke had been a vampire surprised her, but pleased her, too. She enjoyed nothing more than killing one of them. As she ate she sat on the edge of the bed and looked across the room and into the bathroom where Stoke now lay dead. Becka couldn't help but wonder how many more vampires were out there searching for Blake. Like her own kind, vampires had become skilled at hiding themselves in plain sight amongst the humans. Stoke had even fooled her, and she him.

Not knowing how many more vampires were searching for Blake and wanting to reach him before they did, Becka picked up the piece of Moonbeam Stoke had left on the bedside dresser. She held it in her hand. And just like it had for Stoke, the piece of stone pulsed bright blue when she faced north.

Becka smiled to herself. Stoke's phone rang. She looked at it, then placing Stoke's half-eaten heart to one side, she picked up the phone. Staring at the screen, she read the name Josef, flashing across the front. Switching the phone off, she crushed it underfoot. Once dressed again, Becka slid the fragment of Moonbeam into her pocket and left the room and Stoke behind her.

Chapter Twenty-One

"Answer!" Josef screamed at the phone held tight in his fist. His voice echoed off the walls of the vast chamber beneath the Carpathian Mountains. It made his voice sound like that of a young girl.

"Is there a problem?" he heard his master ask.

Josef spun around, unaware that King Nicodemus had joined him. He'd always found his king's ability to sneak up on him – appear out of nowhere – disconcerting. Now as he turned to face his king and his blood red stare, Josef found the fact that he had suddenly appeared terrifying.

"There is no problem," Josef told his king, his voice uneven and weak.

Nicodemus almost appeared to glide across the vast barren chamber toward him. His long crimson robes fluttered, yet there was no breeze – no wind in the caverns beneath the mountains. "So you have news for me?"

Josef drew a quick, shallow breath as he stood before his master, head slightly bowed so as not to look into his eyes. He couldn't bear the anger and the pain he saw in them. He knew the pain was for the death of his daughter, Frances, and the anger for him.

"My brother is close to capturing the wolf," he said.

"Close?" Nicodemus asked, the grief in his soul now intolerable. "You said that before, Josef."

"But it's different this time," Josef dared to explain. "My brother caught up with the wolf. They fought…"

"And?" Nicodemus interrupted. "Tell me! Tell me! Does he have the wolf's head?"

Dropping to his knees, Josef gripped his king's robes. Still unable to look him in the eyes, he began to wail. "My brother has a piece of the Moonbeam, my liege. Not all is lost yet. We just need to give Lance a little more time. Blake will no longer be able to conceal himself from my brother… from us… from *you*… there is no place now for him to hide."

"You and your brother have had enough time!" Nicodemus screamed, his rage threatening to overspill again. His eyes swivelled red in their sockets as tears of blood started to form in them. His white face began to twist and writhe. The maze of wrinkles contorting his face out of shape with hate.

Fearing that time had run out for him, Josef cradled his king's legs. They felt thin and brittle beneath the overflowing robes. "The wolf heads north," he sobbed in one last feeble attempt to save his own life.

"Why?" Nicodemus asks.

Josef shook his head. He daren't say that he didn't know the answer to that question. But Nicodemus believed that he knew why the wolf might be heading to the north. Nicodemus knew that the wolf's father once owned a house in a remote part of Scotland. Could it still be there after all these years? After so many wars? After the wolves had been hunted into extinction? If it was, perhaps Blake was heading there. But why?

"I'm sorry," Josef sobbed, his arms still wrapped about his king's legs. Bending low, and on his knees, he brushed aside Nicodemus's robes. He looked at the king's feet and grimaced. Each was long, bony, and white. They looked more like a raven's claws than human feet.

"I'm sorry for failing you, my liege," Josef whimpered. "I'm sorry for being such a coward." With his nose just an inch from the cracked stone floor of the chamber, he kissed his master's feet.

"Perhaps it is I who has been the coward?" Nicodemus said, his voice now suddenly soft – almost understanding – caring.

He lowered himself to the floor so he was at the same level as his servant. He took Josef's face in one twisted claw and raised his head, so that for the first time since coming into the chamber, they had eye contact.

"Coward, my liege?" Josef mumbled, his face stained with tears. "I don't understand."

"Perhaps it should have been me who went in search of this wolf." Nicodemus smiled into his servant's face. "Frances was my daughter, after all. It was I who truly loved her. It is only I who feels pain at her loss..."

"We all feel the pain..." Josef wept.

"Shhh," Nicodemus soothed. "Perhaps I feared leaving my home where I am safe and know the wolves can't reach me. Perhaps it should have been I who went after the wolf all those hundreds of years ago, instead of sending my precious daughter. If I had found the courage to go, then she would never have met Thaddeus Blake. She would never have loved him. Frances would still be at my side now."

"But..." Josef said, wanting to tell his king that he wasn't a coward and that it was the wolf that was to blame for Frances's death.

"No buts," Nicodemus said, taking his servant in his arms. "It is time that I left the safety of these mountains and went and avenged my beautiful daughter's death."

"Then let me travel at your side," Josef said. "Let me..."

A red ribbon of blood gushed from his mouth. The last thing he saw was his king's unforgiving stare, as his head toppled from his shoulders.

Nicodemus pushed the headless corpse away and stood up.

"I will do what you and so many others have failed to do," Nicodemus seethed at the headless body at his feet. "I will rid the world of the last remaining wolf."

Nicodemus's robes spun all around him as he glided back across the ancient room. They fell away to the floor, leaving nothing in its place but a black column of smoke. The smoke floated upwards and out of the chamber.

Chapter Twenty-Two

On the outskirts of Glasgow the train began to slow. Thaddeus eased open the carriage door and peered out. It was beginning to get light. Tracks snaked away in both directions. Thaddeus knew he would need to find a place for Winnie to shelter for the day. He knew too that he would have to find some fresh meat for her. As the wind ruffled his unkempt hair, he thought he saw the perfect place for both of them to rest for the day.

"Give me your hand," he said, looking back into the carriage at Winnie. She came forward and took hold of his hand.

"Thanks," she said.

"For what?"

"Listening. I've never told anyone what happened to me and Ruby... what we did at that orphanage," she said.

Gently squeezing her hand, he said, "If it's any comfort to know, I would have killed Duvall too. But I wouldn't have hung that piece of filth. I would have ripped his throat out."

"I love you," Winnie said.

"I love you right back," Thaddeus smiled, then lept from the train, taking Winnie with him.

From the cess they watched the train head toward Glasgow railway station. Once it was gone, and under the cover of the fading darkness, Thaddeus led Winnie along the tracks. His leg hurt less now, just a dull thud where only hours before there had been an explosion of pain. In the distance they could see the bright overalls of track workers and trains being shunted slowly back and forth.

"In here," Thaddeus said, stopping outside a disused signal box and forcing the door.

They stepped inside into the welcoming darkness. A strip of approaching daylight shone through one grubby window and Winnie shied away from it back into the shadows. Her skin prickled and her stomach began to ache with hunger again. She looked about the old signal box as Thaddeus searched for something to place over the window. There was enough space on the floor for them both to lie down. Against the far wall was a set of levers protruding from the floor. They were covered with a thick coating of cobwebs. Winnie guessed that it was these levers which would have been used to change the points in the tracks outside. As she inspected them, Winnie could see that someone had written the words *PUSH* and *PULL* on the wall above the levers in white chalk. The words had faded a little.

"Do you think I should *push* one?" she asked, glancing at Thaddeus.

He looked back at her. "I wouldn't if I were you."

"Why not?"

"They might still be connected to the tracks outside," he said, dragging a large piece of tarpaulin out from beneath some chairs that had been stacked in one corner.

"But they look so old," Winnie said, gripping one of the levers.

"Shhh!" Thaddeus suddenly said. "What's that?"

"What?" she whispered back, hand still on the lever.

"I can hear music," he said.

Winnie cocked her head. She could hear it too. "Sounds like that song *Heroes* by David Bowie," she whispered.

"Get down, somebody must be coming," Thaddeus said, tugging at Winnie's sleeve.

She let go of the lever and the music suddenly stopped. "Whoever it was must have gone," she whispered.

"Probably one of those track workers looking for a place to take a leak," Thad said, crouching and peering through the window. Satisfied that he couldn't see anyone, he placed the tarpaulin over the window, showering the signal box in darkness.

Winnie sat bolt upright on the floor of the signal box. Thaddeus had gone from beside her, but she could tell that she wasn't alone.

"Who's there?" she whispered into the darkness.

As if in answer to her question, a small hooded figure stepped forward. And although it was close to black inside the signal box, she knew that it was Ruby Little who was now standing before her.

"Ruby?" Winnie said.

She felt a cold hand slide over hers. "Come with me, Winnie, I've got something to show you."

Getting to her feet, Winnie said, "Are you going to show me through the monster's eyes again?"

"Yes," Ruby whispered, leading her friend toward the door.

"But I don't want to see through them," Winnie said, pulling a little on Ruby's hand.

"You must see," Ruby said, pulling open the door, "or you will never truly understand."

"Understand what?" Winnie asked, stepping through the doorway and out onto the tracks. But she wasn't on the tracks. She was nowhere near the railway. She looked back and the signal box was no longer there. Nor was Ruby. Winnie was in a deep wood, and where the signal box had once been was now the abandoned police car she had fled from with Thaddeus. It was covered with branches and leaves just how she remembered it to be. Winnie could hear a noise. It was a banging sound. She stepped forward, realising that the thumping and banging was coming from the boot of the police car.

Placing one foot slowly in front of the other, she made her way toward the car. The sound of the banging grew louder with each step she took, drowning out the noise of snapping twigs beneath her feet. With her heart racing, Winnie stood before the boot.

"I can't breathe," a voice wailed from inside the boot. "Please let me out."

Winnie reached for the catch on the boot. She stopped. Her hand was no longer her own, but a claw. She knew that she was seeing through the monster's eyes again. This is what Ruby wanted to show her. She watched the claw lift the boot. She recognised the policeman huddled inside. He peered upwards and began to scream as he looked upon the monster. Then, as if unable to control the arms of the creature she was trapped inside, Winnie watched in horror as it tore the police officer to pieces. The attack was frenzied and unrelenting. Strips of flesh, hair, teeth, and entrails splattered the inside of the boot until it was drenched red. Over the sound of the police officer's dying screams, Winnie heard another sound. Someone was approaching through the wood. She turned and saw a figure watching from the darkness beneath the trees.

"Hey, Winnie," the voice said.

"Who are you?" Winnie screamed from deep within the monster.

"Wake up, Winnie," the voice said. "Wake up. It's me Thaddeus..."

Winnie opened her eyes. Thaddeus was shaking her awake by one shoulder. She looked up at him, feeling confused and disorientated. There was light in the room, yet the tarpaulin still covered the window. She looked past Thaddeus and could see that he had found and lit a small oil lamp.

"It's okay, Winnie. You were just having a nightmare," he whispered. Thaddeus held up one fist to reveal several stringy pieces of bloody flesh.

With images of that dead police officer still vivid at the front of her mind, Winnie turned her head away, despite the hunger she felt.

"You must eat, Winnie," Thaddeus told her, offering the meat again. "If you don't, you might still yet die. You haven't changed fully – you're not a true vampire yet."

"When then?" she asked, face still turned away from him. "How much longer will I have to eat this shit for?"

"Forever, Winnie," Thad said. "Your hunger will never fade – your thirst will never be quenched. But it's more important than ever that you eat now or you will fade – you will die. Your soul still lingers in that darkness that is between life and death."

Unable to rid her mind of the nightmare and what Ruby had shown her, Winnie turned her head so as to face Thad. "What kind of meat is it? Is it human?"

"I thought we'd been through this before," Thad said. "I don't eat humans."

"But Ruby showed me..."

"Ruby is *dead*," Thad cut over her.

Winnie looked at him as if he had struck her.

"I'm sorry," Thad said, slumping back against the signal box wall. "I never meant it to sound like that. But you've got to let go of Ruby. You can't go torturing yourself like this. I understand how much Ruby meant to you, and I'm so sorry that she died the way she did, but nothing can change that now, Winnie, like nothing will ever bring Revekka or Frances back to me. All I'm trying to say is that you are going to live for a very long time – forever. You're immortal now, like me. You are going to love many people during the course of your life and all of them will be human. You will watch them age, wither away, and die. That's the curse of immortality. You will be surrounded by death but never experience it yourself. Sometimes I wonder what is worse. To watch the ones you love die, or to die yourself."

"But I keep seeing her," Winnie said.

"You are going to have to learn to let go of those you loved or you'll be haunted by ghosts forevermore," Thaddeus said, offering Winnie the meat again.

Reaching out, Winnie slowly took one of the strips that dangled between his fingers. Thaddeus sat and watched silently as she ate. When she'd finished, she wiped blood from her lips. The thirst in the back of her throat didn't burn quite as much, and her stomach had stopped somersaulting for now.

"It was rat meat," he smiled.

"Piss off," she said.

"Seriously," he half-smiled. "It was all I could find."

"I think I'm gonna puke," Winnie grimaced.

"Not now at least," Thad said, standing up and brushing down his jeans. "While you were asleep I visited some of the pubs around the station. I've managed to get ourselves a lift up into the highlands with a couple of fishermen that are taking a boat to the coast. They're not going exactly our way, but it will be close enough."

"Is our journey nearly over then?" Winnie asked, standing up. "Have we nearly reached the home of your friend Karl?"

"We should be there before dawn," he said, blowing out the light.

Hand in hand, they made their way along the tracks. Together they scrambled up a steep embankment. There was a hole in a fence that they climbed through and out onto a road.

"This way," Thaddeus said, setting off down the street, hoping that by dawn he would be in possession of the Moonshine.

Chapter Twenty-Three

With her foot pressed flat against the accelerator, Becka Horton raced north along the motorway. She had placed the chink of Moonbeam in front of her on the dashboard. It pulsated a brilliant blue, glowing brighter and brighter as she crossed the border into Scotland. She used the Moonbeam to guide her like some supernatural SATNAV or compass.

It started to rain, driving into her car and beating off the windshield. Becka flipped on the wipers and sat forward in her seat, eyes fixed on the road ahead. Knowing that she was now closer than she had ever been in catching up with Blake, she felt a nervous – or perhaps excitable – twinge in her gut. She gripped the steering wheel tight and dared to press down harder on the accelerator. She left the motorway, taking a quieter road. She continued to head north. Always north.

Her police radio was on the passenger seat, and it whined and hissed as it searched for a signal. Garbled messages started to filter through. With eyes still fixed ahead, she took one hand from the wheel and reached for the radio. She twisted the knob on it from left to right. It made a whiny noise before the voices became clear enough for her to hear. She listened to the chatter that passed between British Transport Police on the tracks just outside Glasgow Railway Station and the police control room. Becka turned the volume up so she could hear what was being said over the sound of the rain and wind hammering against her car.

"...that's a negative... the deceased hasn't been struck by a train..." one of the officers on the ground said into the radio.

"What is the exact location of the deceased...?" the control room asked back.

"...the body is still partially wearing his orange track safety clothing and he has been wedged up behind a disused signal box..." the officer reported.

"...and what are the injuries...?" the controller asked, her voice crackling through the radio.

"...erm..." the officer started as if trying to find the right words to describe what he was looking at. "...I can only describe the deceased as looking as if he has been mauled by a pack of wild dogs...or some other large wild creature."

There was a long silence that was filled only with static.

"...please repeat your last message..." the controller spoke again.

Becka didn't need to hear any more. She knew who was responsible for the killings and she was getting closer to him. Reaching for her radio, she fumbled to turn it off. It slid from between her fingers and down into the footwell of her car. Taking her eyes from off the dark winding roads that she was now on, she reached down, fumbling for the radio. Her fingers brushed over it. But it was gone again – out of reach.

"Shit!" she snapped, looking up at the road again, then screaming.

She slammed on the brake with both feet, shooting forward in her seat. Her face hit the steering wheel and she cried out. Feeling dazed, she looked back up, wondering if she had been mistaken by what she had seen standing in the middle of the desolate country road. But she hadn't. The man she had seen standing in the centre of the road was now walking slowly toward her. In the dazzle of the headlights, she could see that his face was lined and scored with age-defying wrinkles. He wore an immaculate black suit and wide-rimmed black hat. She watched him approach the car, the warm sensation of blood running from her split lip.

At the car, the old man pulled open the passenger door and climbed inside.

"What the fuck...?" Becka gasped.

"Shhh," the old man said. Rainwater dripped from the brim of his hat and the end of his long nose. He glanced at her, his eyes red and bright. "We need to talk."

"About what?" she asked.

He reached for her face with one long emaciated hand. It was as white as chalk and wrinkled. Becka flinched backwards but she was not quick enough. He drew one hooked finger along the curve of her lower lip, mopping up the blood that was there. With his finger glistening red and wet, he licked her blood from his finger with his black tongue. "Just drive," he said, smacking his bloodless lips together.

Looking front, he smiled at the sight of the Moonbeam pulsating blue and white on the dashboard.

Chapter Twenty-Four

Thad and Winnie stood in the dark and watched the two fishermen drive their van away into the distance. They had made better time than Thaddeus could have hoped for. There were still three hours or more until first light, which was more than enough time for them to make their way on foot across country to Karl's home.

Winnie stood by the grass verge and watched the taillights of the van disappear into the darkness. The conversation between them and the two fisherman had been light. The two guys seemed nice enough, but she was constantly mindful now of what she said and to whom. After about half an hour or so of both Thaddeus and Winnie giving one word and guarded answers to the fishermen's questions, they gave up trying to make conversation and listened to the radio instead. Before they had driven away, Thad had taken some of the money from the envelope he had given to Winnie, along with the passport, directions to his home in Italy, and Frances's passport. The driver took the money with thanks, leaving Thad and Winnie alone beside the desolate road.

"Feeling fit?" Thad asked Winnie.

"I guess," she shrugged. After the meat Thaddeus had given to her in the signal box, her hunger and thirst had subsided. She felt stronger now than she had the day before and the day before that. Perhaps her change from human to vampire was almost complete? She wondered.

"Have you still got the gun?" he asked.

"Yes," she nodded, placing her hand to the small of her back and feeling the cold lump of metal tucked into the waistband of her jeans. "Why, do you think we're gonna need it?"

"Let's hope not," he said.

"But I thought you said Karl would help us," Winnie reminded him.

"He blames me for killing his daughter Revekka, remember?" he said back.

"That was hundreds of years ago," Winnie said.

"Such time passes in a blink of an eye when you're immortal. I guess we will never know how Karl feels unless we get going," Thad said, taking her hand in his. "Ready?"

Winnie nodded, her fiery red hair turning black and green eyes shining blue again. Thad noticed that she could change her appearance with ease now and he suspected that it wouldn't be too long before she was raven-haired and blue-eyed permanently. And just like she had changed, so now did Thad, his hair growing thicker, his stubble darkening, eyes blazing bright. With claws entwined with each other, they turned toward the barren moorland that stretched before them and raced away into the night.

Winnie ran faster than she had ever had. Glancing down at her feet, she could see that they were nothing more than a blur. She moved so fast it was like the world around her had slowed down – as if it couldn't keep up with her somehow. Thaddeus raced along beside her, never letting go of her hand. She squeezed his fingers with her own and he smiled sideways at her. As they ran, Winnie lost all sense of time and distance. How much ground had they covered? Was it five miles, ten, twenty, even? How fast did they move and what other supernatural powers would she develop as she changed fully from human to vampire? It was as she raced like this with Thad at her side, feeling free, her long rich black hair billowing out behind her, eyes so bright that she could see through the very night, that Winnie wondered if she really had been cursed. Wasn't the chance of spending an eternity with Thaddeus a gift?

Together they raced over hills, through valleys, racing streams, and forests. The moon sat crescent-shaped above them, peeking out from behind cloud that scudded over it. How long until the next full moon? Where would she lock Thaddeus away? Perhaps in the same place that Karl locked himself away from the world. But if he had such a place, who locked and unlocked him?

Reaching a coastal path, Winnie began to slow. Not because Thaddeus had, but because she suddenly felt as if her newfound strength was ebbing from her. Thaddeus slowed his pace, too.

"Are you all right?" he asked, noticing that her hair and eyes were turning back to their original colour.

"I'm just feeling a bit weak," she said, stopping near to a cliff edge. She bent forward, drawing in deep lungfuls of sea air. Waves crashed against the black rocks below.

Thad placed one arm about Winnie's shoulder, pulling her close, away from the edge. "I probably pushed you too hard," he said.

"No, it's okay," she breathed deeply. "I wanted to. It was fun. I enjoyed it."

"I wished now that I got those fishermen to drop us closer to Karl's," Thad said. "I thought you were strong enough to make the last part of the journey on foot."

"That's kind of you, Thad," she smiled, kissing him gently on the cheek. "But I'm stronger than you think."

"Okay," he smiled back, taking her hand in his again. "We can walk the rest of the way. The house isn't too far from here."

Thaddeus changed once more as he walked beside Winnie toward the house his father had once shared with Karl. To any casual onlooker, Winnie and Thad would have looked like any other young couple who had just fallen in love. The coastal path led them for about another mile along and around the cliff edge. As they walked, it had started to rain. Winnie glanced down at the writhing waves below as they churned about the jagged rocks. Looking up, she could see a lighthouse. It stood on a giant bed of black rock that jutted from the sea. Waves smashed against the rocks showering the sides of the lighthouse. It stood in the shadow of a giant cliff. On the very edge of it, Winnie could see a house.

"There it is," Thad said pointing through the wind and the rain. "That's the house." He looked up into the sky and sensed that they had at least two hours before daybreak. That gave him enough time.

Together, side by side, they approached the house. It was in darkness. No lights shone within. Winnie couldn't help but wonder if the house was deserted – that Karl had moved on. She glanced at Thad and could see that his eyes were fixed on the house as they approached it through the rain and the dark. Waves broke against the rocks below, sounding like thunder. As they drew closer still, Winnie could see that the house was bigger than perhaps she first thought. The building was white and pristine – not shabby looking. There was a tidy looking front garden with flowers and crab apple trees. Each of the windows was lattice in design, and one or two of them had coloured glass making the house look like a small church. The roof was thatched and a brick chimney jutted from the top of it.

Reaching the front door, they both stopped. Winnie looked at Thad, then back at the house. Both listened for any sound, but all they could hear was the *boom boom boom* of the waves and howl of the nagging wind.

Making a fist, Thaddeus knocked on the door.

They waited.

Thaddeus knocked again.

A light flickered on in the passageway on the other side of the door. The sound of slow, deliberate footsteps. They heard a bolt being thrown and keys jangling in a lock.

Slowly the door swung open. A thickset man filled the doorway. He had white bushy hair that would have looked more at home framing the face of a mad scientist. His face was ruddy in complexion with a firm jawline.

He stared long and hard at Thaddeus with a bright pair of hazel eyes. "I always knew someday you would darken my home and life again, Blake," Karl Lauderdale said.

Chapter Twenty-Five

"You better come in," Karl said, stepping aside. His voice was deep and gruff. Winnie couldn't be sure if this was how he usually spoke or whether he was just pissed off at seeing Thaddeus at his door. Karl wore a blue dressing gown and slippers.

Thaddeus and Winnie shot each other a look, then both stepped inside. They found themselves in a narrow passageway that led into a wider hall. The floor and walls were made of stone. There was a staircase leading upwards. On the floor was a rug. The walls were not decorated, apart from one oil painting. It was of a beautiful looking girl and was set in a thick gold frame. Thaddeus stopped and looked up at it, his eyes dark, face taut. Winnie guessed that the girl in the painting was Revekka, the first girl Thaddeus had loved.

"Remember her, do you?" Karl grunted, catching Thaddeus staring up at the painting.

"How could I ever forget," Thaddeus whispered.

"Forgotten what you did, 'ave you?"

"I haven't come looking for trouble…" Thaddeus said, looking away from the picture and back at Karl. Winnie noticed that Thad's eyes looked as if tears were threatening in them. She wanted to go to him, but she didn't. She knew that these were old scars that she couldn't heal. Only Thaddeus and Karl could do that between themselves.

"You were always trouble," Karl sniffed.

"I killed my own father protecting Revekka," Thaddeus shot back at him. "Remember that?"

"You end up killing everyone you say you've ever loved, Blake," Karl spat, his voice brimming with anger. Then, glancing over at Winnie, he added, "I'm surprised Frances is still alive. I'm surprised you haven't killed her yet."

Winnie looked back at Karl, then away again.

"Hang on," Karl breathed deeply, taking a step toward Winnie. He took her by one arm and led her into the light of a nearby lamp. He looked closely at her face. "You're not Frances."

Winnie gently eased herself from his grasp. She had no quarrel with this man. She hoped, like Thaddeus did, that Karl would be able to help them. "My name is Winnie," she said.

"Then you have killed Frances, too," Karl gasped, turning on his heels to stare at Thaddeus.

"It wasn't my fault," Thaddeus was quick to explain. "Our maid released me too soon – she set me free and as a wolf I bit Frances. No one feels that anguish more than me."

As if he hadn't heard Thaddeus, Karl said, "But the truce. The agreement you had with Nicodemus and the vampires – you've broken it. They will come looking for you. They will come in search of the last of the Lycanthrope..."

"They are already looking..." Thaddeus started.

"But I am like you," Karl said, staring at Thaddeus, mouth open. "They do not know about me... I've lived here in peace... in secret..."

"That's why I'm here..." Thaddeus tried to cut in, desperate to explain.

"But if they are after you then they might have tracked you here... to me..." Karl gasped in horror. Then racing across the hall, he gripped Thaddeus by the arm. He yanked him back toward the front door. "You must leave. You must get as far away from me as possible. Get out! Get out, I tell you! Get out!"

"Listen to me!" Thaddeus shouted, pushing Karl back from the open door. "I've come for the Moonbeam. We can use it to stop the vampires once and for all. I just want to live in peace. That's all I want. That's all I've ever wanted."

"If that's all you've come for, then take it," Karl said, racing back across the hall and up the stairs. "Take it then get out of here. Get as far away from me as possible."

Winnie watched Thaddeus run after Karl, then followed. Wind blew in through the open doorway as if chasing her up the stairs. At the top, she found herself on a wide landing. Winnie watched Thaddeus follow Karl into a room. She headed down the landing and into the room after them. It wasn't a bedroom, but a study. There was a long wooden desk with a leather-bound chair on the other side of it. On the desk was a laptop, some books, a decanter of wine, and one single glass. The walls were lined with bookcases, each of them crammed full of finely bound books. They looked old and some of the spines were worn. So many old books gave the room a musty kind of smell – like an ancient library. A window was set into the wall. It was ajar and Winnie could hear the waves crashing against the rocks below again.

Winnie and Thad watched as Karl rummaged through the desk drawer. Crumpled pieces of paper shot into the air as he frantically searched. His hand fell over what he had been looking for. With key in hand, he ran across the study. A painting was fixed to the wall. But this one wasn't of Revekka but a vast snow-capped mountain range. Winnie wondered if this had once been his home before the vampires had chased the werewolves from it.

Karl lifted away the picture, placing it carefully on the floor. Set into the wall where the painting had once been was a safe. With a shaking hand, Karl thrust the key into the lock. He twisted his wrists and the safe door fell open. Reaching inside,

Karl took out a folded piece of muslin cloth. It looked old and dirty.

"Take it," he said, offering it to Thaddeus.

As if taking hold of some ancient religious relic, Thaddeus took the cloth from Karl. He opened up the piece of material and looked wide-eyed down at the Moonbeam. Winnie took a slow step forward into the room and looked into Thaddeus's hands.

"Wow," she breathed.

"Isn't it the most beautiful thing you've ever seen?" he asked, mesmerised by the Moonbeam.

In the hands of a wolf, light radiated out from the centre of the stone and sprayed the walls. Shafts of blue and white light sparkled in the air. "This will bring us peace at last, Karl," Thaddeus said, still staring down at the Moonbeam. "This will stop the vampires."

"But you need the Moonshine," Karl reminded him.

"Do you have it?" Thad asked, glancing up.

"It doesn't work," Karl said.

"So you do know where the Moonshine is then?" Thad asked.

"It doesn't matter whether I do or I don't, the Moonbeam and Moonshine don't work when put together."

"Where is the Moonshine?" Thad demanded to see it. "Let me try."

"You're wasting your time..."

"Where is the Moonshine?" Thad asked again. "Just tell me."

Winnie and Thad both watched Karl raise his arm and point out of the open window. They both looked in the direction he was pointing. All either of them could see was the silhouette of the lighthouse in the distance. "There stands the Moonshine," Karl said.

"The lighthouse?" Winnie asked.

Karl slowly nodded his head. "The Moonshine – the prism – is set in the top of the lighthouse," Karl began to explain. "When you place the Moonbeam inside the prism, legend says that invisible rays of moonlight will shower the Earth, killing all vampires. But yet it doesn't."

"How do you know?" Thaddeus asked.

"Because I tried it," Karl said. "I feared that time like now might come and I would need to protect myself. But it doesn't work. It's almost as if something – some small part – is missing."

Looking down at his hands, Thaddeus turned the Moonbeam over. He found the small crack where that one small piece of Moonbeam had broken away all those hundreds of years ago. "I know what's missing," Thaddeus half-smiled to himself.

"What?" Karl asked, eyes wide with hope.

"This," Thaddeus said, reaching up to his ear only to find that the piece of Moonbeam was gone. "Where is it?"

"Where's what?" Karl asked, sounding baffled.

"The missing piece," Thaddeus cried, searching his pockets. Realising that he had lost it, he looked at Winnie, eyes wide and full of fear.

"Where is it?" Winnie asked, feeling his panic.

"I have it," a voice said.

All of them spun around to find Becka Horton standing in the open study doorway.

"You?" Thaddeus gasped.

Chapter Twenty-Six

"You're the police officer I saw in the woods," Winnie said, fearing that the police had finally caught up with her and Thaddeus. "She showed me her badge. Her name's Sergeant Becka Horton."

"She's not a police officer, and her name isn't Becka," Thaddeus snarled, still holding the Moonbeam. "Her name is Dominika and she is my cousin."

"And I've been hunting you since the day you deceived me and my mother in those woods," Dominika said. "My mother died because of you and you murdered the man I loved."

"Don't give me that," Thaddeus scoffed. "He wasn't a man, he was a thieving piece of shit and so were you and your mother. You stole the Moonbeam from my father. You drove him half mad then tried to terrorise me from my home."

"And it was you who killed my daughter," Karl scowled at Dominika, stepping forward and standing shoulder to shoulder with Thaddeus, like there had never been any feud between them.

"You got what you deserved. Now give me that piece of Moonbeam," Thaddeus instructed her.

"I don't think so," Dominika said with a sly smile, opening her fist to reveal the shard of Moonbeam. It flashed in the palm of her hand.

Both Thaddeus and Karl leapt across the study at her, claws out and jagged teeth bared. But Dominika was too quick for them. Knocking Winnie away and back into the corner of the room, she sprang toward the open window. Holding the piece of

Moonbeam between her thumb and forefinger, she thrust her hand out of the window, dangling it high above the crashing waves below.

"Come any closer and I'll drop it into the sea," she warned them. "I promise I will do it and it will be lost forever. How will you ever defeat the vampires then?"

"You're a wolf," Thaddeus reminded her. "The vampires will kill you too."

"I don't think so," she smiled back at them. "I've struck a deal that will keep me safe forever."

"A deal with who?" Karl growled.

"With me," a voice said from behind them.

Both Thaddeus and Karl turned around, while Winnie stared on from the corner of the room. She hadn't seen the old looking man, who now sat in the leather back chair at Karl's desk, enter the room. It was like he had simply appeared there.

"Nicodemus," Thaddeus hissed, one claw raised, the other gripping the Moonbeam. Both Thaddeus and Karl now looked half man and half wolf. The old man continued to sit impassively in the chair, one leg crossed over the other, long slender hands folded in his lap. From the shadows, Winnie couldn't help but feel the atmosphere in the room growing more hostile with every passing moment. It was almost suffocating. Everyone in the room had at least one reason why they wanted Thaddeus dead. Karl seemed to be on his side at the moment, but Winnie had come to understand that allegiances between Thaddeus and his kind seemed to change from one moment to the next. Winnie wasn't sure who she could trust, and she guessed that Thaddeus felt just the same. Closing her eyes and making fists with her hands, she tried to search deep inside of herself. She looked for the creature, for the vampire she knew lurked inside. She wanted to draw her out so she could fight to protect Thaddeus if he needed her to.

She would not let him stand alone. She loved him. But however much she tried to bring the vampire to the fore, she couldn't. She was still too drained from the run she had made with Thaddeus – it was like her strength had been sapped from her.

"And you really believe *he* won't kill you?" Thad hissed back over his shoulder at Dominika. "He wants us all dead. That's all his kind has ever wanted."

"No one can want you dead more than me!" Dominika shouted back, her face creased with anger. "You killed my mother. You killed my lover."

"Anyone who helps me kill you will be rewarded," Nicodemus said, pushing the chair back and standing up. Then looking hard at Thaddeus, eyes burning red, he screamed, *"I just want your fucking head!"*

For someone so thin and frail-looking, Nicodemus sprang over the desk in one quick leap, driving Thaddeus back across the room. From the shadows, Winnie watched in horror as Thaddeus was thrown back off his feet, crashing into the wall on the opposite side of the room. Brick and plaster showered down all around him like there had been some explosion. Thaddeus dropped to the floor as Nicodemus lunged for him again.

"You killed my precious daughter!" Nicodemus screamed, fresh red tears of blood leaking down his gaunt, pale cheeks. He sunk his claws into Thaddeus's unkempt hair and yanked back his head, exposing his neck. "I trusted you, wolf, with my daughter's life. I entrusted you with the one thing I treasured more than life itself. I let you live, and how did you repay me? *You killed her!*"

Karl shot forward to help his friend, if that's what Thaddeus was to him. But before he had taken more than two quick strides forward, Dominika had sprang away from the wall, claws out, raking them down Karl's back. He howled in pain, turning and forcing her backwards across the study with his own claws. Dominika flew over the desk onto the floor.

With his mouth at Thaddeus's neck, lips rolled back to reveal his fangs, Nicodemus sneered and said, "This is so easy. I thought Thaddeus Blake the wolf would have put up more of a fight than this."

Still hidden by the shadows in the corner of the room, Winnie raised her hands to her face. She willed them to change, to become claws so she could leap from the darkness and save Thaddeus, who appeared just moments from having his throat ripped out by Nicodemus. But knowing she was running fast out of time, Winnie stepped from the shadows and confronted Nicodemus, vampire or not.

"Leave him alone," she said, trying to make her voice as loud and as threatening as possible, even though her legs were screaming at her to turn and run. But she wouldn't run and leave Thaddeus alone. She was in love with him and she couldn't imagine anything ever changing that. Nicodemus looked up to see who it was that was brave – or stupid –
enough to order him to let the wolf go. He took one look at the young woman who had stepped from the shadows and dropped to his knees, his claws releasing Thaddeus.

"Frances?" he whispered, looking up at Winnie. "Frances, is that really you? I thought you were dead."

Winnie looked at him and understood who he believed her to be.

Crawling on his hands and knees, he went to her. Gripping hold of her legs with his brittle fingers, Nicodemus pulled himself up. Holding her tight to him, he cried out, "It is you. Tell me it is you, my blessed Frances."

Winnie wanted to pull away from him. She didn't want to be in his arms when he realised that she was not his daughter.

Winnie could only imagine his heartache and anger. And knowing that it was only a matter of time before he discovered that he wasn't cradling his precious daughter, and wanting to be strong enough to have any chance of defending herself, she sunk her teeth into his neck. He shuddered against her. Blood pumped into her mouth, washing down the back of her throat. His blood was hot and bitter. She gulped as much as she could before Nicodemus pushed her away from him.

Pulling one hand to the puncture marks in the side of his neck, Nicodemus felt his blood trickling between his fingers. Screwing up his red eyes, he looked at the girl standing before him. Her bite didn't feel like that of a true vampire. He also knew that no vampire would dare feed from him – not even his own daughter.

"What is this trickery?" he seethed, clawing at the air in rage. "Who is the girl who looks so much like my daughter that she deceived even me?"

Winnie felt his blood hit the pit of her stomach, then spread like fire through her veins. Glancing down at her hands, she saw her fingers stretch, grow longer, more slender than she had ever seen them before. She ran the tip of her tongue over her front teeth and felt the jagged points there.

Looking straight at Nicodemus, Winnie said, "I'm sorry that your daughter is dead, but I am not her. My name is Winter McCall. I'm in love with Thaddeus Blake and I'm a vampire, just like you."

"A vampire!" Nicodemus screeched, blood streaming from his eyes in rage. "No true vampire could bring themselves to love a wolf."

"Your daughter did. Perhaps she understood that vampires and werewolves could find love. Live in peace with each other," Winnie said.

"Don't you mention my daughter's name, wolf lover!" Nicodemus screeched, swiping one claw through the air, sending Winnie flying backwards across the room. Feeling as if she had been dropped from a giant height, Winnie hit the floor and cried out. Looking through her long black fringe, she searched for Thaddeus.

Nicodemus sprang toward her, his uncontrollable rage now fully fixed on her. "Thaddeus, help me!" Winnie screamed.

She watched as Thaddeus sprang to his feet, but instead of coming toward her, he raced toward Dominika. Howling, he leapt on her, claws slicing through the air. She cried out, the shard of Moonbeam flying from her fist. Seeing it, Thaddeus snatched the flashing piece of stone out of the air. Looking more wolf than man now, Thaddeus threw himself at the window. With the window frame splintering like matchwood and showering the room in glass, Thaddeus leapt out of the window and onto the rocks below. He raced across them, desperate to reach the lighthouse and the Moonshine now that he finally had both pieces of the Moonbeam in his claws.

Chapter Twenty-Seven

Roaring so loud that the whole room seemed to tremor in its ancient frames, Karl bounded into Nicodemus, sending the vampire king flying back across the room and away from Winnie.

"I had no idea what you were," Karl said, yanking Winnie to her feet with one bristling claw.

"So are you going to kill me now that you know I'm becoming a vampire?" Winnie asked.

"I don't know yet what kind of vampire you might turn out to be," he said. "You look like Frances and that might not be where the similarities end. I have hope..."

"Look!" Winnie said, before he'd had a chance to finish what he'd wanted to say. "They're going after Thaddeus and the Moonbeam."

Karl spun around to see both Nicodemus and Dominika leap from the window and out into the night. "You go after the girl," Karl said. "Leave Nicodemus to me."

Then he was gone, leaping across the room in one giant bound and disappearing out of the window. With eyes shining bright, raven black hair swishing about her shoulders, Winnie sprang up onto the window ledge and out into the night.

Landing with a thud, Winnie rolled over. She was at the very edge of the cliff. Staring down into the darkness, she could see Thaddeus racing over the rocks. Black waves continued to crash against them as both Nicodemus and Dominika chased after him. Nicodemus moved at a terrifying speed as he scrambled over the rocks. He had torn free his jacket and shirt, and his body was white and sinewy. Wispy tendrils of grey hair streamed back from his narrow skull in the wind. Dominika raced over the rocks, bending forward on all fours and propelling herself forward. Both were nearly upon Thaddeus. With Nicodemus's blood still racing through her veins like liquid fire, Winnie scrambled down the cliff face, her long claws striking groves into the hard rock. Halfway down, she threw herself clear, spinning through the air. Landing with poise, she sprinted forward over the rocks. Just ahead she could see Nicodemus and Dominika about to strike as Thaddeus ran and scrambled over the rocks toward the lighthouse.

Within striking distance of Thaddeus, Nicodemus raised his talon-like claws, then shot sideways through the air as if he were nothing more than a leaf caught on a gust of wind. Karl howled as he spun through the air with Nicodemus in his claws. They landed on the rocks, the sounds of bones breaking unmistakeable over the roar of the wind and crash of waves. Even though both were wounded, they got to their feet almost at once. Nicodemus dived at Karl, his claws slicing through the air so fast that they were little more than a blur. Blood and flesh shot into the air like some kind of grotesque confetti. Karl howled in pain as the vampire slashed and ripped at his body.

Winnie continued to speed over the rocks after Dominika. Ahead she could see Thaddeus. The Moonbeam flashed so brightly in his claws now that it lit up the night sky like streaks of lightning. He reached the stone steps that led up to the lighthouse. A giant wave broke over them, smashing into Thaddeus. He fell, dropping to his knees. Dominika saw this and struck out at him.

"No!" Winnie screamed, hurtling herself through the air at the wolf. Winnie sunk her claws into Dominika's sides. The wolf threw her head back, giant jaws snapping just an inch from Winnie's face. Winnie jerked backwards, taking Dominika back onto the rocks with her. Over her shoulder, Winnie saw Thaddeus stagger to his feet, then clamber up the stairs toward the door of the lighthouse.

"You stupid bitch!" Dominika screamed, tussling Winnie onto her back. She leant over the girl, drool swinging from her cavernous jaws and down onto Winnie. "Don't you realise? Blake will kill you too."

"Never," Winnie yelled back, raking her claws in the air, desperate to rip out the wolf's throat – to shut her up.

"Then die," Dominika howled, throwing back her head and sinking one of her claws deep into Winnie's side.

Winnie screamed in agony as the wolf's claws sunk into her flesh like five red hot knives. The pain was too much to bear. Winnie put her hand to the pain. She gripped Dominika's wrist, desperate to pull the jagged claws from her side. It was then her fingers brushed against something cold and hard digging into her back. Gritting her teeth against the pain, Winnie curled her fingers around the gun and yanked it free from her waistband. Dominika had her head thrown back as she howled, sensing that the vampire lying beneath her would soon be dead. Pressing the gun to the fur under her chin, Winnie looked away, then pulled the trigger. The gun exploded in her fist, making her arm recoil violently. Winnie cringed as she felt something sticky and hot splatter her face. She eventually dared look back up at Dominika and gagged. One side of her face was missing. Her brains dripped onto Winnie. Screaming in disgust, Winnie heaved the body from her. Crawling away, she watched Dominika roll over onto her side. As she did so, the wolf took on her human form once more. Winnie looked down at the semi-naked girl lying on the black rocks one last time before a wave crashed over the body, dragging it into the sea.

Winnie glanced over the rocks in search of Karl. Was he still alive? Where was Nicodemus? Had he killed Karl and slipped into the lighthouse while she'd been fighting with Dominika? Waves swept up all around her, some as tall as buildings. Bent forward, Winnie raced toward the stairs that led up to the door of the lighthouse. Reaching them, she heard a scream. Winnie looked back to see Nicodemus racing toward her. His eyes shone so bright they looked like they were leaking fire from deep within his skull. His thin lips were twisted into a tormented snarl as he lept through the night at the young vampire girl, claws shining like daggers. Winnie raised the gun and took aim. With her finger on the trigger, the gun was suddenly snatched from Winnie's hand. She glanced left at the wave that had taken it.

"No!" she screamed, forced back onto the stone steps by Nicodemus.

She felt the wound in her side tear and she crunched up in pain, drawing her knees up to her chest. Nicodemus loomed over her, blood running from his mouth and eyes. He drove one bony foot down into Winnie's face. She felt her fangs puncture the inside of her mouth as it filled with her own blood. He drove his foot down again, this time into her arm. Winnie heard one of the bones break with an eye-popping snap. He drove the heel of his boot down onto the fracture.

Winnie screamed in pain.

"You can make the pain go away," Nicodemus said. "Just join me and help kill the wolf."

"Never!" she screamed as he dug the heel of his boot down onto her broken arm again.

"As you wish..." Nicodemus started, then suddenly stopped with mouth hung open.

He looked at Winnie as if suddenly in shock, eyes wide before his head rolled forward, plopping down into her lap. Winnie looked up to see Karl standing behind Nicodemus's headless corpse. Panting and soaked with blood, he pushed

Nicodemus's body off the steps and into the sea. He then collapsed onto his knees.

"Karl," Winnie gasped, knocking the head from her lap with a grimace. It rolled away down the steps, where at the bottom it bounced into the sea.

"If I were you, I'd get to Thaddeus and tell him Nicodemus is dead before he uses the Moonbeam and kills all of the vampires... you included," Karl said, collapsing onto his side.

Chapter Twenty-Eight

With her remaining good arm, Winnie pulled open the door to the lighthouse. It was narrow and circular inside. A staircase spiralled upwards. She could hear the sound of running feet – Thaddeus racing up the stairs above her. The sound of his foot falls on the stone steps echoed back at her like gunshots.

"Thad!" Winnie called up the stairs, her voice sounding weak, the pain in her side and arm still blinding. Winnie staggered to the foot of the stairs. "It's over. Nicodemus is dead."

He made no reply. Biting her lower lip, she began to climb the stairs. Just lifting one foot and putting it in front of the other was agony.

"Wasn't I meant to heal quickly now that I am a vampire?" Winnie cursed. But am I yet fully turned? She wondered.

Gasping for breath at each step she took, Winnie made her way upwards. Several times she paused to call out to Thaddeus. To tell him that it was all over. That Nicodemus was dead. But not once did he answer her.

Eventually, Winnie could see the top of the staircase. She gasped with relief, gripping the handrail. She pulled herself upwards, taking deep breaths with each step. At the top, she staggered out into a circular chamber. The walls were made of glass. At its centre, where there should have been a light, was a pillar of stone. It looked something close to a sundial – a moon dial perhaps? she thought. On top of the pillar was what looked like a glass flower, with its petals open. Thaddeus stood before it. The Moonbeam and the smaller piece in his hands. He no longer looked like a wolf, but the man she had fallen in love with.

"Thaddeus," Winnie gasped, staggering forward.

He glanced up at her, hands holding the Moonbeam hovering over the open glass prism.

"It's over," Winnie said, shuffling forwards, near to collapse. "Nicodemus is dead and so is Dominika. You're safe."

"I'll never be safe while there are still vampires," he said, holding the Moonbeam over the Moonshine.

"But I'm a vampire, Thad, and I would never hurt you," she said, looking at the Moonbeam and then at him again. "I love you..."

"I'm sorry, Winnie," he said, lowering the Moonbeam into the Moonshine.

"But if you place the Moonbeam into the Moonshine, then I will die. You told me that," she said, her lower lip wavering and eyes filling with tears. "You said you wanted a truce."

Looking down, Thaddeus placed the Moonbeam into the Moonshine. He held the last remaining piece between his thumb and finger.

"Please don't, Thaddeus?" Winnie gasped, out loud. "You're breaking my heart. After everything we've been through together...after all that we've shared..."

Unable to look at her, Thaddeus dropped the final piece of the Moonbeam into the Moonshine.

Winnie dropped to the floor like her legs had been chopped away below the knee. "No!" she screamed as a thousand rays or more of bright blue moonlight shone out from the centre of the Moonshine. The light was so bright in the confines of the chamber at the top of the lighthouse that she lost sight of Thaddeus. From outside she could hear the scream of the wind as it circled the lighthouse. Eyes closed, and lying on her side, all she could see was utter darkness. It was impenetrable – like a wall. And from behind it she thought she heard the wind again. But it was as Winnie lay and listened, knees pulled up to her chest, she realised that it wasn't the scream of the wind she could hear, but the cries of agony coming from the throats of dying vampires. Looming out of the darkness that engulfed her, Winnie could see them in their hundreds and thousands crumbling away to nothing but ash. The wind took them, scattering them like dust.

She waited for the moment that she too would be scattered. She peered into the darkness and saw her friend Ruby Little. Was she waiting for Winnie - to take her across to the other side? Winnie knew she had come to save her – just like Ruby had saved her from Duvall. And Winnie felt an agonising twist of pain in her heart. But it wasn't because she was fading – disappearing on the wind like ash. It was the guilt she felt at not having been able to save Ruby. She had died alone just like Ruby's friend Brian in that derelict farmhouse.

"I'm sorry, Ruby," Winnie whispered, her friend coming out of the darkness. "I'm sorry."

"Shhh," Ruby whispered, leaning over her. "You have nothing to be sorry for, Winnie. You were my friend – the very best friend that I ever did have. But you have to be strong now."

"Why?" Winnie asked.

"Just open your eyes and you will see…" Ruby smiled from beneath her hood, her face as beautiful as it ever was.

"See what?" Winnie asked.

But Ruby was gone. Disappearing again just like she had so many times before.

Slowly, Winnie opened her eyes. She was lying on the floor of the circular chamber at the top of the lighthouse. The bright blue rays of moonlight had gone, but the wind still roared outside. Thaddeus stood at the pillar where the Moonshine sat. He couldn't mask his surprise at seeing Winnie open her eyes.

"Winnie?" he said coming away from the pillar towards her.

She looked up into his face, then shuffled backwards away from him. "Get away from me!" Winnie cried out. "You tried to kill me..."

"No!" Thaddeus said, dropping to his knees beside her. "It was my plan all along."

"What plan?" Winnie asked, still keen to keep her distance from him. Could she trust him? That was something she now doubted. The pain in her side and arm continued to make her feel sick. Her mind swam back and forth as she tried to deal with the pain and uncertainty she now felt.

"I knew the Moonbeam wouldn't kill you," he said, reaching for her, wanting to pull her close.

She shrugged him away. "How did you know?"

"Because you hadn't fully turned," Thaddeus said. "You're not a true vampire yet."

Winnie looked at him, deep into his eyes. Was he telling her the truth?

"He didn't know that," a voice said.

Both Winnie and Thaddeus looked back towards the staircase. Karl was standing at the top of them, bent over in pain. He looked at Winnie. "He's lying to you, Winnie. There's no way he could have known that for sure. Even if he'd suspected such a thing, he was willing to risk your life to find out..."

"Shut up," Thaddeus snapped, jumping to his feet. "You'll say anything because you still blame me for Revekka's death. You hate me."

"I don't hate you, Thaddeus," Karl said, with a shake of his head and tears in his eyes. "I just hate how you use people to save yourself."

Turning, Thaddeus looked back at Winnie. "Don't listen to him. He's a liar. I love you, Winnie. I haven't used you."

"You used me," a little voice whispered from the corner of the room. They all turned their heads to see Ruby Little step from the shadows.

"Ruby?" Winnie gasped, pulling herself up onto her knees.

Ignoring her friend, Ruby stepped across the chamber, stopping in front of Thaddeus. She pulled back her hood. Her face was decomposed and maggot infested, just how Winnie had seen Ruby in her nightmares.

At the sight of her crawling face, Thaddeus lurched backwards. "You're dead. Dead! Dead! Dead!"

"You should know," Ruby said, maggots spilling from her mouth and down the front of her bright red coat. "It was you who killed me."

"Wha…" Winnie croaked, so shocked and confused she was unable to form one simple word.

"Tell Winnie how it was you who gave me the drugs that killed me," Ruby said, looking up at Thaddeus who seemed almost to cower before her.

"No…" Winnie stammered, clawing herself up the lighthouse wall to her feet. Her legs felt like rubber and she feared they might just buckle beneath her at any moment. "Tell me it's' not true…' she groaned, staggering towards Thaddeus. "Please tell me it's not true…"

Thaddeus looked away. He said nothing.

"He arrived in a taxi just before you got back to the Embankment that night, Winnie," Ruby said, the flesh about her mouth cracking as she spoke. "He gave me the drugs. He told me they were free. He told me they would take the cold and hunger away…"

"No!" Winnie cried, stumbling forward and striking Thaddeus over and over across his face. "You murdered my best friend…"

"I did it for you, can't you see that," Thaddeus said, gripping Winnie's wrists. "I did it to help you."

"Liar!" Winnie screamed, yanking herself free of him. "You did it for yourself. All of this – *everything* – has been about you."

"I did it to save you…" Thaddeus started.

"You killed Ruby to save yourself," Winnie spat at him. "You knew I wouldn't have left London without my friend. So you killed her. If she was dead, I had no reason to stay. I was free to leave London with you."

"She was dead already," Thaddeus shouted back, the veins in his neck standing out. "She had no life on the streets. Neither of you did. If it hadn't have been me who gave her the drugs, she would have overdosed on somebody else's sooner or later. I saved you from the same fate. I saved your life, Winnie."

"No, you saved your own," Winnie hissed at him. "You used me like some kind of fucking shield. I bet you couldn't believe your luck when I got bitten. I bet you thought the vampires would leave you alone if you travelled with a vampire. That's the only reason you let me tag along."

"No!" Thaddeus barked. "Okay, so I killed Ruby and used you – but that was at the start. I was desperate. Yes, I wanted to survive and I would have done anything to stay alive – but things changed – my feelings changed. I fell in love with you, Winnie."

"You're a murderer," Winnie screamed, clenching her fists so tight that her fingernails cut the palms of her hands. "You killed Ruby to save yourself."

"We are more alike than you think," Thaddeus said back.

"What the fuck are you talking about?" Winnie snapped.

"It was you, Winnie, who killed the man and his wife back at the farm. It was you who killed the cop in the back of the police car. And you probably don't remember yet, but you killed a railway man..."

"You're a liar..." Winnie gasped.

"Tell Winnie the truth," he said glancing at Ruby. "She told me you've been letting her look through the eyes of the monster, but you never told her who that monster really was, did you?"

"Ruby?" Winnie gasped, now looking at her decaying friend.

"I was trying to show you what you were becoming," Ruby said softly.

"It's not true..." Winnie gasped in horror.

"It is true," Thaddeus said. "I came back from hunting food on the farm and found you in the farmhouse. You were sitting at the table as if in some trance. You had killed the farmer and his wife. After returning from searching for food in the wood, I found you shredding the cop in the back of the car. Again it was like you had been sleepwalking. The same with the railway man. You killed those people to survive, Winnie. You needed blood and you went looking for it. Just like I killed Ruby to survive, so did you. That makes us the same."

"No it doesn't," Karl said, limping forward in pain. "You could've stopped her. You could've chained the girl up – secured her – just how we lock ourselves away on each full moon. But you didn't because you knew that this day might well come and you wanted to be able to make Winnie believe that she was the same kind of monster as you. While she was going under the change, she had no idea what she was doing. She wasn't in control of her actions no more than we are when fully turned. You knew that. You could have saved those people. It's not Winnie who has their blood on her hands, but you, Thaddeus."

"You bastard!" Winnie screamed launching herself at Thaddeus.

He took her by the arms again.

"I've done what I came here to do," Thaddeus said, staring at her. "Whatever you might think about me, Winnie, I do love you. I did what I had to do to survive. It's all I've ever known. All I've ever done is survive. But apart from you, the vampires are all dead now. We could have a chance – we could have a life together. The vampires and werewolves could finally have a truce – find peace."

"And what about me, Winnie?" Ruby whispered. "I can't truly die unless the wolf who killed me dies too."

"Don't listen to her..." Thaddeus started.

"What Ruby says is very true," Karl said, his many wounds dripping blood onto the floor. "Any person killed by a wolf will walk the Earth as one of the undead. Slowly decomposing – decaying – until the wolf that killed them dies too."

Winnie looked at Thaddeus, then at Ruby. She saw Ruby running along the landing, rushing to save her from Mr Duvall. She saw Ruby lying dead in the gutter. She remembered wanting to save her – the guilt she felt for not saving Ruby, like Ruby had once saved Winnie. Winnie looked back into Thaddeus eyes. She saw herself and him running hand in hand, feeling free for the first time in her life. She saw them making love, holding each other tight, feeling truly loved – deep feelings of joy like she had never felt before.

Thaddeus looked into Winnie's bright blue eyes. They were blue again, no longer green. Her hair was black. God, she looked so beautiful...

He felt a sudden pain, like a set of red hot pokers sinking deep into his chest. He felt fingers curl around his heart. Thaddeus broke Winnie's stare and looked down. Winnie's fist was buried in his chest. A black circle of blood had formed around it.

"But you can't kill me..." he murmured, blood forming at the corners of his mouth. "You love me...remember..."

"You killed my friend," Winnie whispered in his ear. "And I hate you for doing that."

Kissing him gently on the mouth one last time, she closed her claw around his heart, yanking it from his chest.

Thaddeus slumped forward into her arms. She let his lifeless body slide to the floor. With tears streaming down her blood stained cheeks, she turned to face her friend. She looked upon Ruby's face, which was once again as beautiful as she remembered it to be.

"Thank you, Winnie," Ruby said, rushing forward and holding Winnie tight.

Winnie hugged her back. Both friends stood at the top of the lighthouse, the sound of their sobs drowned out by the scream of the wind from outside.

"Don't be sad, Winnie," Ruby whispered.

"You're crying too," Winnie said softly.

"These are happy tears."

"What have you got to be happy about?"

"Because I've got the best friend that anyone could have ever wished for," Ruby said.

Pulling Ruby closer still, Winnie held onto her friend. "I don't want you to go. I don't want to be alone."

"You won't be," Ruby said, easing herself from Winnie's arms. "That's a promise."

Winnie stood and watched, as Ruby pulled her bright red hood back up over her head. Karl stepped away from the wall, and hobbled towards Winnie. He looped one giant arm about her shoulders, pulling her gently against him. Together, they stood and watched Ruby Little turn and head back across the chamber, where she disappeared once more into the shadows.

Chapter Twenty-Nine

Together, Karl and Winnie made their way back across the rocks to his home that almost seemed to balance on the very edge of the giant cliff. With both of them injured and in pain, their progress was slow. As the first rays of sunlight speckled the sea like glitter, Karl was ushering Winnie back into his home and out of the sunlight.

He led her upstairs to a room at the end of the long landing. Winnie saw the bed on the other side of the room and just wanted to fall into it. With his arms still about her shoulders, Karl helped her across the room. Letting out a groan of pain, then pleasure, Winnie rolled onto the soft mattress.

"Okay?" he asked kindly.

"I guess," she shrugged just wanting to close her eyes – wanting to forget what had happened and what she had learnt. She hoped that she might wake up and her world would be different. What kind of world Winnie hoped for she didn't quite know.

"Get some rest," Karl said, pulling a blanket up under her chin.

He turned and limped back toward the door.

Winnie called after him. "Karl, will I always want to kill people?"

"Not if you choose not to," he said, looking back at her. "We all have a choice. Even Thaddeus had that."

He closed the door, leaving Winnie alone in the darkness. Within moments sleep had taken her.

Winnie woke. It was dark. At first she felt a little disorientated. Reaching out she found a bedside lamp and switched it on. She was in the room Karl had led her to. How long she had slept, Winnie had no idea. But as she sat up in bed, she noticed that she was no longer in the filthy clothes she had once been wearing. Winnie was now wearing a pretty white nightdress. Who had changed her clothes, she wondered? She tenderly pressed her side where Dominika had skewered her. There was very little pain now. Just a dull ache. Carefully, Winnie pulled up her nightdress and could see that a piece of white gauze had been placed over it. Someone had been looking after her. It was then Winnie noticed that her arm wasn't crippling her with pain. She bent it at the elbow, then flexed it straight again. There was no pain at all. It was as if her arm had mended itself while she had slept.

Swinging her legs over the side of the bed, Winnie stood up. She felt a moment of wooziness, but it passed. A chair had been placed at the end of the bed. There was an open book lying face down on it. Somebody had been sitting in her room and reading as she'd slept. She glanced down at the title. It read, *The Sydney Hart Mysteries*. There was a dressing gown draped over the foot of the bed, so snatching it up, Winnie threw it on and left the room.

On the landing she smelt the waft of roast beef seeping up from below. Her stomach leapt at once, and the thirst returned. Winnie made her way downstairs, following the scent of the food. On the opposite side of the hall, she pushed open a door to reveal a wide kitchen. There was a long wooden table at its centre with chairs gathered around it. A fire roared in a nearby hearth. Karl was standing at a worktop and carving a large joint of beef into thick bloody slabs. Hearing the door open, he glanced up.

"Hey, Winnie," he beamed. "Take a seat. You're just in time for supper."

Winnie sat at the table, the smell of the meat maddening. "How long did I sleep for?"

"Three days," Karl said.

"Really?" Winnie asked, sounding surprised.

"You were really bent out of shape," he said, crossing the kitchen towards her, holding a plate of meat. He placed it on the table. "Eat up and keep your strength up."

Winnie glanced down at the thick slices of meat. It was still very red at its centre and swam in a pool of blood. She thought of the meat that Thad had brought her – of the meat she had gone hunting for herself.

As if being able to read her mind, Karl said, "You don't have to worry, Winnie, that's nothing but the best Scottish beef. There ain't anything better."

Winnie picked up a nearby knife and fork and cut herself a piece of meat. As she forked it into her mouth, Karl placed a steaming bowl of vegetables down onto the table. "Help yourself," he smiled.

Winnie sat and watched Karl busy himself as he placed dirty pots and pans into a large sink.

"Have I fully changed now?" she asked him.

"How do you feel?" he asked taking a seat at the table and heaping some of the food onto a large round plate. He pushed a jug of milk towards her.

"I feel great," Winnie said, pouring herself a glass.

"Then I guess you're over the worst," he said. "But if I were you, I'd take things easy for the next few days."

They sat and ate in silence, the sound of Karl's jaws chomping up and down almost deafening.

"What happened to Thaddeus?" Winnie finally asked.

"You know what happened to him," Karl said, pushing more of the meat onto the back of his fork.

"What I mean is, where is his body?"

"Oh, I see," he said. "I've buried him. I did it while you were asleep. I thought it was for the best. I'll take you to see his grave if you like – if it would help."

"Okay," Winnie said, looking back down at her plate. She didn't feel hungry anymore. Then looking at Karl, she said, "You seem much better. Have you healed okay?"

"Yes, thanks," he said around a mouthful of food. "I'm not as young as I used to be and any wound or injuries can take a little longer to heal up these days. But they always do."

A gust of wind rattled the window in its frame and sent sparks up the chimney. Winnie glanced up and out of the window. In the darkness she could just make out the silhouette of the lighthouse in the moonlight. She looked back at Karl.

"What do you do on a full moon?" she asked.

"What do you mean?" he asked, putting down his knife and fork.

"Don't werewolves have to lock themselves away during a full moon," Winnie asked. "Don't you need someone to keep watch over you?"

"I watch over him," a voice said from over Winnie's shoulder. "We look after each other."

Pushing her chair back from the table, Winnie looked back to see who it was that had spoken. A girl of about seventeen years stood in the open kitchen doorway. Winnie recognised her at once. It was the girl from the painting in the hallway.

"Revekka?" Winnie gasped.

"Let me introduce you," Karl said, standing up and joining the girl in the doorway. "Winnie, this is my daughter, Revekka. Revekka, this is my friend, Winnie."

"Pleased to meet you," Revekka said with a pretty smile. Winnie could see at once why a man like Thaddeus would have fallen in love with her.

"But I thought you were dead," Winnie said, watching Revekka take a seat at the table. Her father sat next to her.

"That's what we wanted Thaddeus Blake to believe," Karl started to explain.

"Thaddeus' cousin, Dominika, did not kill me," Revekka said. "She bit me, but not fatally. But as my father carried me away in his arms that day, Thaddeus believed I was indeed dead."

"And that's what I wanted him to believe for the rest of his life," Karl said. "Although I once loved that boy like a son, I knew he was selfish, cunning and dangerous. He had already put my daughter in harm's way. Having her bitten by a werewolf was bad enough – I couldn't risk him ever finding out that she was alive as he would've come looking for her. It was better that he and the rest of the world believed Revekka was dead."

Winnie stared at her across the table. For someone who had lived for hundreds of years she looked so young. Revekka wore her thick hair loose about her shoulders and wore very little make-up. She was wearing a sweater and jeans, just like any other young woman would.

Although Winnie already knew the answer to her own question, she still felt the need to ask it. "So are you a werewolf?"

"Yes," Revekka said. "Dominika's bite turned me. As soon as my father discovered what we had both become we fled our homeland and settled here in Scotland. We have lived here in secret ever since."

"So what happens on a full moon – when you change?" Winnie asked.

"We go out to the lighthouse," Karl said. "The full moon brings in the tide and we can't get back to the mainland. There we stay until the full moon passes. We are quite safe and so are the humans."

"Thaddeus did the same thing once or twice," Winnie said.

"It's an old trick, but a good one," Karl said.

Revekka heaped some of the food onto her plate. "So what will you do next?" she asked Winnie. "Where will you go?"

"Thaddeus gave me Frances' passport, some money and the directions to a secret home he had in Italy," Winnie explained. "He bought it for Frances, should she ever need to escape."

"Are you trying to escape?" Karl asked.

"From my past perhaps," Winnie said thoughtfully. "But I look upon it as a fresh start for me."

"When do you plan on leaving?" Revekka asked.

"As soon as I can, I guess," Winnie shrugged, taking another gulp of milk.

"Remember what I told you," Karl said in a fatherly way. "Get some rest for the next few days before you go anywhere."

"I will, I promise," Winnie smiled.

Alone in her room, Winnie showered. With a towel wrapped about her, she stood by the window and looked out at the lighthouse. There was a knock at her door.

"Come in," she said, without looking back. Reflected in the windowpane, she saw Revekka enter her room. She was carrying something in her hands.

"I thought you might need these," she said, crossing over to the bed.

Winnie stepped away from the window and watched Revekka lay some fresh underwear, jeans and a sweatshirt onto the bed.

"Was the nightdress yours too?" Winnie asked.

"Yes, a bit too small to be my father's," she smiled.

"Was it you who looked after me, while I slept?"

"Yes," Revekka nodded. "I sat in the chair over there and read, so I could keep an eye on you. I wanted to make sure that you were going to be okay."

"Why?" Winnie asked. "You don't even know me. And I'm a vampire. Aren't we meant to be enemies?

"Are we meant to be?" Revekka said. "All I know is that it gets incredibly lonely around here sometimes – like most of the time actually. I've had a few human friends over the years but they've never known – you know – what I really am. But they either move on with their lives and move away or grow old and die. I've seen so many friends die that it kind of hurts too much to find a new one."

"That's really sad," Winnie said.

"Sad for the both of us," Revekka reminded her.

"I guess."

"Anyway, I won't bother you," she said, heading back toward the door.

"You're not bothering me," Winnie said.

"Really?" Revekka smiled, turning around. "You don't mind if I stay and chat for a while?"

"Knock yourself out," Winnie grinned, picking up the fresh clothes.

Revekka flopped down onto the bed. Winnie sat next her.

"Thaddeus told me all about you," Winnie eventually said. "He told me how much he loved you."

"He had an odd way of showing it," Revekka said, not with bitterness, but with a sense of regret.

"Perhaps he didn't really mean to hurt either of us," Winnie said.

"Is that what you hope or what you believe?" Revekka asked.

"I'm not sure," Winnie said looking back towards the window so Revekka couldn't see her eyes and the tears in them.

"Can I ask you something?" Revekka smiled.

"Sure," Winnie said sniffing back her tears and hoping that Revekka didn't notice her doing so.

"I know you're keen to leave here, but will you stay until the day after tomorrow?" Revekka asked.

"Why?"

"It's a full moon tomorrow, so me and my father will head out to the lighthouse at sundown. We'll come back the day after, but will sleep for much of that. I'd like to say goodbye before you go. Like I said, it's not often, if ever that I have someone my own age about the place to chat too."

"I'll wait for you," Winnie said, touched by her suggestion.

"You promise?"

"I promise."

Winnie did keep her promise. The following evening as it grew dark, Winnie watched from her bedroom window as Revekka and Karl made their way over the rocks to the lighthouse. It wasn't long before she heard deep booming howls coming from the rocks. Winnie knew it wasn't the wind or the waves crashing against them that she could hear. From her window she sat and watched the hulking shapes of the two wolves scramble back and forth over the rocks as they howled up at the moon.

Winnie ate some of the meat that Karl had prepared for her. She wandered alone about the house and could only begin to imagine the isolation and loneliness that Revekka had described to her. Putting on some boots and a coat she found hanging by the door, Winnie left the house. In the dark and with the wolves howling up from the rocks below, Winnie went in search of

Thaddeus' grave. She hadn't gone very far when she found it in a small field behind the house.

Karl had made a cross and placed it at the end of the grave, which was covered with pretty white and purple flowers. These she guessed had been placed there by Revekka. Without saying anything, Winnie sat on the ground beside the grave of the man that part of her still loved and in some way understood. With head cast forward, Winnie sobbed, until the first rays of sunlight crept over the cliffs in the distance.

Winnie slept through until full dark. On waking she knew that she had to go. She had kept her promise to Revekka and would say goodbye before she left. The constant sight of the lighthouse had too many memories for her – none of them good. She wanted to put some distance between them and her. After showering and getting dressed. Winnie placed the envelope stuffed with money in her back pocket, along with Frances' passport and the directions to the house in Italy.

Winnie looked back into the room just once, then closed the door behind her. She headed back downstairs to the kitchen. Revekka was at the table, wrapping some meat up in sheets of greaseproof paper.

She looked up at Winnie. "So you're leaving then?"

"Yes," Winnie nodded, not wanting to meet Revekka's stare.

"I've put a parcel of food together for you." Revekka said, placing it into a rucksack on the table.

"Thanks, Revekka," Winnie said, taking if from her.

As she did, Revekka grabbed her hand. "Let me come with you."

"What?" Winnie asked, surprised.

"Take me with you, Winnie," Revekka said. "I've packed enough food for two."

"It's not the food," Winnie said, easing her hand from Revekka's.

"What is it then?"

"We're not the same," Winnie said. "I'm a vampire and you're…"

"I know what I am," Revekka said. "But how can we both be so different. We've both loved the same man."

Winnie looked at her, fighting the urge to say yes.

"I'm not going to change for at least another twenty-eight days," Revekka said. "That will give us plenty of time to get to Italy, find the house and a place for you to look out for me…we could look out for each other."

"I don't know…" Winnie said, feeling herself weakening.

"You told your friend, Ruby, that you were scared of being alone," Karl said stepping into the doorway.

Winnie turned to face him. "And what about you?"

"What about me?" Karl shrugged his broad shoulders. "I can look after myself."

"Won't you miss, Revekka?"

"With all my heart," he said, going to his daughter and taking her hands in his. "But for too long my daughter has been nothing more than a prisoner here. But Thaddeus Blake is dead now and his death gave birth to my daughter's freedom. I just want her to be happy. Such a remote place is not fit for a young woman."

Winnie looked at Karl then at Revekka. "I guess you better go and get packed," she grinned at her.

"Already done," Revekka squealed, reaching beneath the table and pulling out another rucksack.

Karl stood in the open doorway as both Revekka and Winnie stepped out into the cold. Winnie could see that however happy he appeared to be, he fought back tears at his daughters leaving.

"I love you," Revekka said, leaning up on tiptoe and kissing her father's cheek. He held her tight, lifting her feet from off the ground.

"I love you more," he whispered and put her down again.

"Thanks, Karl," Winnie said, stepping forward and kissing Karl's cheek. "Thank you for everything."

He took one of her hands in his. Winnie felt him slide something into the palm of her hand. She opened it, looked down at the chink of Moonbeam that had been fashioned into an earring.

"Just in case," he whispered.

"In case of what?"

But instead of answering, Karl stepped back inside his house and closed the door. Heading down the path with Revekka at her side, Winnie fixed the piece of Moonbeam to her ear.

With stars shining brightly overhead, Winnie and Revekka set off down the coastal path together. One werewolf. One vampire. A new beginning for both species. And the start of a new friendship and new adventures for both of them.

The End.

More books by Tim O'Rourke

Kiera Hudson Series One

Vampire Shift (Kiera Hudson Series 1) Book 1
Vampire Wake (Kiera Hudson Series 1) Book 2
Vampire Hunt (Kiera Hudson Series 1) Book 3
Vampire Breed (Kiera Hudson Series 1) Book 4
Wolf House (Kiera Hudson Series 1) Book 5
Vampire Hollows (Kiera Hudson Series 1) Book 6

Kiera Hudson Series Two

Dead Flesh (Kiera Hudson Series 2) Book 1
Dead Night (Kiera Hudson Series 2) Book 2
Dead Angels (Kiera Hudson Series 2) Book 3
Dead Statues (Kiera Hudson Series 2) Book 4
Dead Seth (Kiera Hudson Series 2) Book 5
Dead Wolf (Kiera Hudson Series 2) Book 6
Dead Water (Kiera Hudson Series 2) Book 7
Dead Push (Kiera Hudson Series 2) Book 8
Dead Lost (Kiera Hudson Series 2) Book 9
Dead End (Kiera Hudson Series 2) Book 10

The Kiera Hudson Prequel Series

The Kiera Hudson Prequels (Book 1)
The Kiera Hudson Prequels (Book 2)

Kiera Hudson Series Three

The Creeping Men (Kiera Hudson Series Three) Book 1 Coming 2014!

The Jack Seth Novellas

Hollow Pit (Book One)
Seeking Cara (Book Two) Coming 2014!

Black Hill Farm (Books 1 & 2)

Black Hill Farm (Book 1)

Black Hill Farm: Andy's Diary (Book 2)
A Return to Black Hill Farm (Book 3) Coming 2014!

Sydney Hart Novels

Witch (A Sydney Hart Novel) Book 1
Yellow (A Sydney Hart Novel) Book 2
Raven (A Sydney Hart Novel) Book 3 Coming 2014!

The Doorways Trilogy

Doorways (Doorways Trilogy Book 1)
The League of Doorways (Doorways Trilogy Book 2)
The Queen of Doorways (Doorways Trilogy Book 3) Coming 2014!

Moon Trilogy

Moonlight (Moon Trilogy) Book 1
Moonbeam (Moon Trilogy) Book 2
Moonshine (Moon Trilogy) Book 3

Samantha Carter – Vampire Seeker Series

Vampire Seeker (Samantha Carter Series) Book 1
Vampire Flappers (Samantha Carter Series) Novella
The Vampire Watchmen (Samantha Carter) Book 2

The Tessa Dark Trilogy

Stilts (Book 1)
Zip (Book 2) Publishes October 2104

The Mechanic

The Mechanic

Unscathed

Written by Tim O'Rourke & C.J. Pinard

Flashes

Flashes (Book 1)
You can contact Tim O'Rourke at
www.kierahudson.com or by email at kierahudson91@aol.com

Printed in Poland
by Amazon Fulfillment
Poland Sp. z o.o., Wrocław